A NIGHT TO REMEMBER

SWEET AND SASSY SERIES
BOOK 1

YVONNE ELLIOTT

NALEIGHNA KAI

LA2YE PUBLISHING

This is a work of fiction. Names, characters, places, and incidents are products of the author's imagination or are used fictitiously and are not to be construed as real. Any resemblance to actual events, locales, organizations, or persons, living or dead, or somewhere in between, is entirely coincidental.

A Night to Remember @ 2023 by Naleighna Kai and Yvonne Elliott

EBOOK ISBN: 978-1-952871-52-8

Cover designed by: J. L. Woodson jlwoodson@woodsonstudio.com

www.woodsoncreativestudio.com

Interior design by: Lissa Woodson www.naleighnakai.com

Editor: U. M. Hiram

Beta Readers: D.J. Mitchell

ACKNOWLEDGMENTS

All praise and honor to the Creator always. A special love and respect to my guardian angels, ancestors, teachers, and guides.

To my spiritual mothers: Sandy Spears and Bettye Mason Odom; to my son, Jeremy "J. L." Woodson, just when I think you can't up your game, you prove me wrong. I am so proud of you, Number One Son. Much success to you in your graphic design and consulting business. Oh, and I have to add, you put your foot in the cover of this novel!

To the people who continuously have my front and my back:, D. J. Mitchell, Martha Kennerson, Shannan Harper, Jennifer Addison Cole, Aisha Lusk, Jamyi Joy, and Ehryck F. Gilmore; to Janine A. Ingram; to Janice M. Allen (my developmental editor who also has the best ear and doesn't mind giving it to me straight, no chaser); Unique M. Hiram, Martha Kennerson, Stephanie M. Freeman, Margaret "Bunny" Ervin, Royce Slade Morton, La Ammitai, J. L. Campbell, Shakir Rashaan.

Many thanks to Vikkas Bhardwaj for the Hindi translations, information on East Indian culture, and that hot cover image on Loving Me for Me; to Suresh Bhasin for his hospitality and insight into East Indian Festivals; to Lady, Kim, Sankit, Sanjay, and everyone at India House Chicago who have shown me so much love.

To the book clubs and avid readers who support my work—I love and appreciate each one of you.

To everyone I mentioned (and those that I may have forgotten to type), thank you for everything you are to me.

Wishing you all—peace and love, light and joy.
    —Naleighna Kai

DEDICATION

YVONNE ELLIOTT

I dedicate this book to those individuals who never stop challenging me, even when I resist with all my might. This work is dedicated to those who yearn for connection, love, and intimacy. Always remember that life is too short to allow outside forces to tell you who or how to love.
I extend my appreciation to NK's Tribe Called Success for their encouragement, affection, laughter, and support along the way and I am equally grateful to my family and friends who gave me the space to tune out the world and pursue the one passion I hold dear after them.

NALEIGHNA KAI

Sesvalah Renee Cobb Dishman,
I miss you more than you know.

My mother, Jean Woodson
My grandmother, Mildred E. Williams
My brother, Eric Harold Spears
My nieces, LaKecia Janise Woodson and Tanisha Donique Woodson,

a rising star who left us much too soon
Tanishia Pearson Jones, Emmanuel Donnell McDavid, and Priscilla Jackson
To Leslie Esdaile Banks (L.A. Banks)
Octavia M. Butler,
two of the best storytellers the planet had to offer.
To Anthony "Green Eyes" Johnson,
to Derek V. Fields (a fallen Cavalier angel)

CHAPTER ONE

"WITH EIGHT CHILDREN, I HAVE JUST AS MUCH GOING ON AS YOU DO,"
Blue said, trying to rein in her frustration.

"You have *seven* children," Reign shot back.

"I was counting the husband," Blue quipped. "And stay on point
with the conversation."

Reign King had been jarred by the phone's strong vibration while
she sat on a tan micro-suede sofa in a hotel room on day one of what
was supposed to be a staycation. She groaned the moment Blue
Sullivan's name flashed across the screen.

'Today, of all days, what does Blue want? This book was getting good.'

Whenever Blue called, it was always something and most times it
wasn't good. The staycation in Chicago was not supposed to be
interrupted by anything but emergencies and food deliveries. Not
exactly in that order. Then Blue called wanting Reign to make a mad
dash to Atlanta to handle manufacturing meetings because she was
now needed at the advertising expo earlier than scheduled.

"I'm not on the clock today, Blue, the manufacturer won't have the
allergy test for our products for another day or two so until the tests
come in, I'm going on a Southern food crawl, I just started reading a
new memoir that I want to finish *on my staycation turned vacation*. So, I

shouldn't be getting any calls related to the first half of my statement since the second half is the only thing on my agenda."

"I thought we were closer than that," Blue said. "We have to keep our toes in a lot of pools these days. We're almost on the home stretch."

Blue was right. Like Reign, they were both Janes of all trades and had way too much going on. Blue had become involved in the advertising industry when her youngest daughter prepared for college. Much to her husband's dismay. Since she had been forced to marry him at an early age, he had made it his ultimate goal to keep her pregnant indefinitely. He'd be hurt to discover that, with the help of his aunt, Blue had managed to sneak off to a neighboring state to get her tubes tied. Aunt Nora had been the only light in a marriage Blue had no choice but to endure. Now freedom was no longer a fleeting thought—it was fast becoming a reality.

Also against her husband's wishes, Blue had landed a position at an advertising agency though she had no experience whatsoever. Now she was the person to connect people with unique opportunities within the agency and with different corporations that were clients of the agency.

"You're right, Blue. You're more than a partner; more than a friend. What's going on? And please make it quick, my book and a nap are calling. And you know with last minute Mike pulling his usual stunts, I don't get to read for pleasure—ever."

"Okay, my friend who is more like a sister to me," Blue said, knowing full well that Mike, Reign's boss at the law firm, was the king of waiting until clock out time—4:59 p.m. to ask for something that would take at least two hours or more.

Wait, did she say 'like a sister to me'? Uh oh. She's laying it on pretty thick. Must be a huge favor she's about to ask.

"Devesh is here in Atlanta for an event. He injured his leg at the gym trying to help another performer in the fitness center."

Just like Devesh. Always the chivalrous one.

"Sorry to hear that, but what does that have to do with me?"

"He's fine, thanks for asking," Blue said in a wry tone. "But he's going to need some help for a few days in the evenings. I'll be taking the overnight shift. Someone else is on the morning shift."

"I understand, but again, what does that have to do with me?"

Reign shifted on the sofa. "The daughter of the person who was originally scheduled appendix burst so she can't do it."

"Okay, and …"

"And I was thinking since you and Devesh already have a relationship."

"Had a relationship. Key word … *had*."

"I'd offer the assignment to you instead of someone else who might end up star-struck and assaulting the man in his sleep. You know that man is so fine."

Reign's heart rate pulsed with a steady thump that echoed in her ears. Blue, more than anyone, knew how much Devesh had hurt her when his traditional East Indian family threatened to disown him if he continued the relationship with a woman fifteen years older than him. A woman of a totally different ethnic and cultural background. She had misgivings about the age gap early on. Devesh assured her that it would *never* be a problem. So it must have been the latter part that had reared its ugly head. She should have stayed in her lane, kept with her vow not to get entangled with love or anything close to it. Roberto taught her that lesson. Shawn taught her that lesson. Devesh, well, core memory made, and valuable lesson learned. Again.

"I haven't seen him in two years. I'd like to keep it that way."

Blue's pause on the end gave rise to another idea.

"Wait, you're not setting me up, are you?" Reign slid off the sofa and started pacing the living room area of her hotel room. "Is Devesh even aware that you're calling me?

"No, he doesn't know about the swap. I also know that he doesn't trust anyone in his private space, especially overnight. So, I'm sure he'll be fine with you staying. Besides, he's on crutches and in a wheelchair. How dangerous could he be?"

You don't know what that man can do with his tongue.

"What is he going to do? Kick you out of the room?" Blue chuckled. "Will you do it? The company that hired him is paying top dollar to make sure he's well taken care of. They know he brings them a lot of business since he resonates with their target audience—women who can appreciate tall, tan and terrific with a deep voice, bedroom eyes—"

"What are you, his pimp?"

"I'm just thinking you can buy more memoirs. And you are not an escort. But if you get a little pickle tickle out of the deal, I won't say a word."

Reign bit her bottom lip and tried not to laugh at that term when it was actually more of a slap and tickle when it came to Devesh. The money might very well buy more books. And she could put some more money on her Cavalcade of Authors Durabia trip since a great deal of her extra cash had gone into The Native Lady, Blue and Reign's latest entrepreneurial endeavor, involved mixing flowers, herbs, and oils from different native lands. They crafted and tailored them to the region and continent of where their client's ancestors were born. Some of them were grown on the Benally farm owned by the Navajo tribe in Gallup, New Mexico. Those elements were used to make tea, salves, and supplements.

With a lot of research, they had the Native American and African mixtures down, but were now branching out into other counties like India, Ireland, and Morocco. When the two unlikely collaborators who had met at an advertising expo, finally had it all together, they were going to make a fortune branching out into an industry that had been foreign to both of them. They would make a success of things with unique products that would set them apart from everything else on the market.

"Reign, I wouldn't ask, but you know I'm in a crunch here. I need to have someone I trust and someone *he* trusts, and you're already in Atlanta anyway."

It's only a weekend. How bad would it be?

"Alright, I'll do it. Top dollar, huh? But those meals had better be Michelin Star worthy, and my accommodations better be upgraded to a suite."

"Done! I'll let the security team know to have your credentials ready when you get to the main floor," she said. "Meet me there so I can give you the salve I mixed up for him. I got some new flowers and oils native to India I want to try. Should work well since it's where he's from originally."

"You know Devesh is not going to agree to be your guinea pig."

"Girl, just rub it on his leg. He'll take vegetable oil on him as long as you're the one touching him. Or if it's put on the right leg."

"You should've done stand-up comedy. Or is that sit down comedy because no one could under*stand* it?"

"Forget you," Blue said with a laugh.

"What time should I get there? North or South Building?"

Blue gave Reign the rest of the details. Make sure Devesh stayed off his feet, make sure he ate something, give him his pain medication on time and make sure he gets enough rest. Pretty simple. But he was stubborn. He'd overdo it during the day and then wouldn't realize how much of a toll it took on him and pay for it later.

Reign disconnected the call and snatched up the book from the sofa. It was just getting to the part about relationships and listening to one's inner voice. *Rebirth* was spot on about trusting oneself with people. She just wished she had picked up this book before she met Devesh. But if she had to be honest with herself and no one else, it wasn't him she was worried about.

CHAPTER TWO

THE SECOND REIGN CAUGHT SIGHT OF DEVESH STANDING NEAR DEB'S Minis By Me; she realized exactly how much trouble she was in. The trouble that mothers warn their daughters about. The kind of trouble that made people need bail money. Devesh's trouble came with its own zip code, and she was circling that area until she landed.

Reign tried to mix in with the overflowing crowd as she walked past that display of luxury hand-crafted miniatures, but the second Devesh caught sight of her, he halted in the middle of whatever sales pitch he was making, and couldn't take his eyes off of her even though he was surrounded by a sea of women. All he could do was follow Reign with his eyes as though none of them mattered.

The first problem was that Devesh Maharaj was a Bollywood actor and spokesmodel. She was far from the model type or anyone who traveled in those circles. The second issue was his family. Reign sighed, remembering his recount of their reaction, which was something akin to horrified. Despite the odds, their friendship had blossomed into a beautiful love affair. She couldn't have stopped it if she had tried, and heaven knows she tried. The age thing. The ethnic thing. The culture thing. She laid all the issues on the table. Devesh wouldn't hear of any obstacles, at first. The more time they spent together, the more both of their emotional walls fell. In a small way, they were both delusional, ignoring the elephant in the room. Actually, the whole herd.

She ignored his gesture to "come hither" and picked up speed to pass the other booths and rushed toward the entrance. She slid up to her suite to get settled in.

Reign arrived to her shift to receive the turnover from Skye the daytime attendant. She told her that Devesh was on Motrin only per his refusal to take anything stronger, and that he spent most of his time sleeping, so the shift should be pretty easy. He was still in a lot of pain and refused to take doctor prescribed painkillers for fear of the addictions he'd heard so much about. He rested quite a bit and made small talk but avoided any of the painful parts of the equation. No talk of the past. No talk of what his family had done. No talk of what he had done.

But when Blue didn't show up for the late shift, and wouldn't answer calls, Reign prepared to go to her suite two floors up, he said, "It's late, why don't you stay here with me?" He gestured to the opposite side of the bed.

"Oh, that's slick trying to get me in the sack," she replied with a laugh. "Are we doing that one leg on top of the covers thing?"

"Woman, I don't have time to play games when it comes to my feelings for you," Devesh said, and his tone was dead serious. "I want you in the best and worst way. But I have control and so do you. It's late. Rumors could spread if someone sees you leave right now. The lawyers from the Intellectual Property firm you work for are here."

Knowing Devesh wouldn't take his injury seriously if she left. Reign opted to stay. Even though she could have tipped to her room upstairs and grab her pajamas, she remained in her clothes in case someone from the security team did a check on their most prized asset. Reign set her alarm for thirty minutes before the daytime attendant was supposed to arrive.

At one point during the night, Reign woke up to Devesh's hand placed ever so lightly on her hip. It was nice to feel the weight and the strength of his hands on her body once again, even if it was in its most innocent form.

She woke up the next morning to find that she was cradled in his arms and he was sleeping so soundly that she knew this was natural for him. Wanting to be close. She enjoyed it too much. The minute she extracted herself and tipped toward the door, he shifted and called out her name. Her heart constricted and she rushed out of his suite. She didn't stop until she was within the safety of her own suite.

He had called out my name …

Even in his most vulnerable state. Why did that make her hurt even more?

CHAPTER THREE

Reign spent the morning organizing her makeshift office set up to navigate the process of getting the core samples from the manufacturer they planned to contract with to produce large quantities of The Native Lady products. Even though she was on assignment with Devesh, she still needed to monitor her emails and check on her son, Jay. Right as she was about to give him a call, she glanced at the screen and noticed that she had a missed call. Reign pulled up a video app and dialed Jay's number.

After a short pause, her son's handsome face appeared on the screen. "Heeeeeey Mama," he said, giving her a megawatt smile. "How's it going?"

"All is well, son, all is well."

"How's our star patient doing?"

"He's fine, as stubborn as ever," Reign replied, wondering how he knew she was with Devesh. They had remained friends even after the split only because Jay had asked to make sure she was good with it. The promise was that no information about Devesh or Reign would be shared.

"He called me after he injured himself to tell me about the incident," Jay said.

"I'm pretty sure he convinced Blue to set me up. Were you in on it too?" Reign said, slightly annoyed.

"Mama, I would never do that, even though I view Devesh as a friend. Family first. I mean, given the fact that you waited until I was damn near grown to get me a father figure and all that."

"You have a daddy," she shot back. "Too bad he doesn't realize the amazing son he has. That's on him, not you. Besides all that, Devesh maybe could be your brother, but never a dad."

Reign, a single woman who swore she'd remain that way when her son's then twenty-one-year-old father abandoned both of them when she was fourteen. Despite limited experience, she succeeded by purchasing her first home at nineteen and performing well at a law firm that gave her a break. She was certainly better than her child's father who, while still living with and off his mother. The perfect example of "failure to launch" syndrome. She didn't have discretion with men at fourteen, but she'd learned that valuable lesson and tried to steer clear of them now. Only one man had stolen her heart—Devesh Maharaj. Then he surprised her by giving in to his family and shattered her heart in such a way that she still hadn't tried to put the pieces together.

"Oh, come on, Mama," Jay teased. "It could be cool having a dad close to my age. I mean, there's soooooo much he'd have to teach me."

"I don't care how cool you think it is," she countered. "It'll be a cold day in hell before that happens."

"Dang, Mama," Jay said, getting the hint that it was time to stop this part of the conversation. "I get it, but I don't care what age he is. As long as he's legal and you're happy, I'm good. Tell Devesh I hope he gets well soon."

"Is everything alright with you?"

"Yes, Mama, the house is fine. The neighbors are fine. The food is … well, I did polish off the leftovers. Other than that, everything is in divine order."

"You'd better not touch my Maxwell Street Polish."

"No promises," he shot back with a laugh.

"I'm going to spank you."

"I'm getting a little too old for those," he said, laughing even harder.

"Full-grown adults love spankings, so ..."

"Hey!" he snapped, and the laughter died down immediately as his expression went to full on shock. "I think this conversation has taken a turn into the TMI section of the parking lot. Bye, Mama. Love you."

"I love you too, son," she said, and couldn't stop laughing.

AFTER HER CONVERSATION WITH JAY, she took a shower, ordered room service, answered a few emails, and read a few more pages of *Rebirth* before her reminder chimed. She gathered her things and met Blue downstairs to pick up a different salve to take back to Devesh's room for the night.

"So how did it go?"

"I'm still in one piece. He's still in one piece," Reign snapped, wondering why it looked as if Blue had been crying. "But the big question is, where the hell were you last night? You were supposed to take the overnight shift and somehow didn't show up and didn't answer your phone, either."

"I had some family stuff come up," she said, and she actually sounded sincere. "I needed some time to get myself together."

"I'm sorry to hear that, but did your hands stop working, too?"

"Hands?"

"You know, your ability to type. Send a text or an email. Something."

"You're right," she said with a weary sigh. "You're right."

Reign peered more closely at her friend observing the dark, tired circles under Blue's eyes. "Do you want to talk about it?"

"Not right now," Blue said, placing a hand over Reign's. "I'm still sorting through a major lapse of judgment on my husband's part. And his family is pissed at me because I won't accept it."

"Wow, that's intense," Reign said. "What are you going to do with the rest of your time before your shift?"

Reign fished the book from her tote bag and held it up. "I'm going to do what I had planned to do all along. Read a book."

"*Rebirth*, huh?" Blue stroked the matte finishing of the cover. "Didn't think you were into memoirs."

"Normally, I'm not, but this reads like fiction and it's inspirational. And I need it right now."

"So could I," Blue said in a voice just above a whisper and a tear escaped and streaked down her ivory check and fell onto her green blouse. "I truly could."

Reign wrapped her arms around her friend. "I'll make sure to buy you a copy. And I'm here for you whenever you want to talk."

CHAPTER FOUR

REIGN ARRIVED AT DEVESH'S SUITE IN THE EARLY EVENING TO START THE second day of her shift. He'd just returned from physical therapy and the daytime attendant made sure Devesh had showered and changed into more comfortable clothes. He'd been killing it on the convention floor and the execs of Elliott Worldwide were pleased that orders were flying for the client's in for their latest products. All well and fine, except Devesh didn't take the breaks he was encouraged to take, and he had been practically dragging by the end of the day.

Reign arrived just in time to help him get settled into the bed as the day attendant swept towards the door.

"Ah, I'm here too late. I missed the sponge bath portion of today's events." Reign announced, carrying two brown paper bags.

"Ha, ha," Devesh said, adjusting on the bed. "I might be injured, but I'm not that down where I can't bathe myself, woman."

"I may have to make a judgment call on that. Who knows what type of pain meds they have you on?"

"I'm still not taking those," he said. "They swear they're not addictive, but I know what happened with the Oxy people. That will not happen to me. Time heals all wounds."

"Time heals some wounds," she whispered. Devesh's apologetic expression let her know that he knew exactly what she meant. Her heart still bore the scares of his abandonment. The second time in her life when a man had done so.

Reign had tried her best not to put Jay's father's trifling ways on blast and to make sure that Jay had some positive male presence in his life. She'd put him in martial arts because it had a multitude of strong men as mentors, and she'd even landed a big brother for him through the Big Brother Big Sisters of Metropolitan Chicago. She had grown up with a father who went out for a Pepsi and some smokes and didn't return until twelve years later—with another set of children and a mistress in tow. The family had been devastated by his absence when it first happened. With the breadwinner missing in action, the family went so far down, they didn't know there had ever been an "up". Their mother, Thelma, a housewife who didn't have a high school diploma or skills that could hold a job that would support six children, never knew what would happen from one day to the next.

The Latino family next door were in the same state as Reign's family. The father had left the seven of them. They were poor, but not quite on the level of Reign's family. So the two mothers began to share resources and survived that way. That is, until Roberto, the oldest son of the Madera family, fell for fourteen-year-old Reign, and she became pregnant.

Maria Madera was forced to intervene and give Reign a place to stay right after that condition of "get rid of it or I'm getting rid of you" placed by her mother went in a direction Thelma never intended. She had to stand in front of the members of the congregation—and apologize for her sin. The process didn't go well for Reign's mother or the pastor.

Roberto turned out to be more like his father than anyone realized. He had been a grown man, seven years older than Reign, yet he blamed *her* for getting pregnant. He evaded police for years when the State tried to charge him with a crime because she was not of the age of consent. Later, Reign was into an ugly child support battle that waged all the way up until Jay started college. Over the years, he avoided paying child support—switching jobs, taking menial positions, collecting unemployment, becoming a "professional" student, and attempting to terminate his parental rights, to name a few.

Finally, after an experience where Roberto ducked into the bathroom right before a court appearance to avoid having to see his son, Jay told Reign, "Enough! I'll make it on my own. Stop going to court for this. I'm going to be married with my own children, and you'll still be up in this place trying to get what you feel he owes you. Enough, Mama. Let it go. Let *him* go. I'm certainly going to."

And Jay was right. So how did she end up with a man several years her junior? A man of a totally different ethnic background? A man with an overbearing family who did not like where their relationship had landed?

The third time did not become the charm, if the second time was such a complete bust.

CHAPTER FIVE

Reign spent a few minutes taking notes from Skye, the daytime attendant. Judging by the stiff expression and the tense set of his shoulders, the petite Asian woman had spent most of her time trying to woo Devesh over. Blue had been right, and Reign was going to let her know that Skye was causing him more stress than necessary.

After Reign escorted her out the door, he exhaled and fell back onto the pillows. Reign set to work getting herself settled in for the night, then worked the room, adjusting his pillows, checking ice packs and anything he might need. She noticed his menthol rub was running low, so she was glad she made a pit stop on the way over.

"How's your leg?" Reign asked, noting that he was much more relaxed now than when she'd walked in.

"It feels a little better," Devesh answered, "Not as bad as the first day. I feel about sixty percent."

"That's great," Reign said, smiling. "That's a good sign that Blue's salve is *making it do what it do*. Now just stay off of your feet and you'll be back to saving little old ladies at the gym in no time."

Devesh's gaze narrowed at Reign's smart-ass remark. "The only person I'm interested in saving is you. Devesh countered, "Oh and whatever's in that bag. It smells wonderful. What did you bring me?"

"Who said this was for you?" she asked, then froze on her way to the dining room table. "And what did you say?"

"You heard me just fine."

"Saving me from what, exactly?"

"From yourself. You put up walls so high that a man can't get over them. So low that he can't get under it—"

"Wait a minute," she snapped, frowning. "Are you quoting Parliament to me?"

Devesh gave her an ear-to-ear smile. "I'm mean, we're supposed to all be one nation under a groove, right, but ..." At that moment, Devesh's stomach growled—*loud*. "What my appetite really wants you to know is that I'd like to be *Knee Deep* in some of whatever's in that bag from..."

"Paschal's," she said.

Devesh's spirits perked up when he heard the name of the soul food restaurant that was an Atlanta staple that started with two brothers in 1947. Reign had talked about it often, telling him that Aretha Franklin, Dizzy Gillespie, Dr. Martin Luther King, Jr. along with other entertainers, politicians and celebrities had visited; but she'd never had the opportunity to visit at times when the expo was in the city.

"That smells amazing," inhaling dramatically as though he could make the food fly from the bag and into his hands with just that gesture. "I didn't realize how hungry I was until I smelled that delicious food."

"Well, let's get you fed before it gets cold," Reign said, trying to wrap her mind around the fact that he had thrown out something deep, couched it in the words of one of her favorite bands, then moved on as if it didn't matter. Same way he had done with their relationship.

Reign set to work in the suite's kitchenette, plating food from the containers for him, then scooted to a safe corner of the living room to perch on a chaise and eat. He grimaced when adjusting his lower torso, giving deference to his injured leg, so he could partake of a plate of macaroni and cheese, fried chicken, collard greens and corn bread, and sweet potatoes.

Aware that the pain in his leg was giving him problems again,

Reign figured until this expo was over, he wouldn't stay off it long enough for it to heal. *Why did he insist on keeping this assignment when the company could've called in someone else?*

Devesh polished off his meal and tackled dessert while being careful not to put any pressure on an area that would bring more pain. "I apologize for hurting you."

She snapped back to the present. Unable to help herself, Reign's gaze flew to his face. The apology she never expected had slipped past his lips. Shocked at his declaration, strong emotions made it impossible to voice what she truly felt. She waved him off, took a deep breath, and finally summed things up with, "Family is important to you."

"*You* are important to me."

"Could've fooled me," she whispered without filtering the sarcasm. "It's been two years since I've heard from you ... *two whole years,*" she stressed, holding up her fingers and tipping her head to illustrate her point that his memory was a little faulty.

Devesh's intense look almost made her melt, despite her annoyance. "I think there's a reason we're here now—together," he said in a husky voice filled with promise. "This is a second chance."

"Don't read anything into it." She gestured to the icepack he placed on his leg, meaning that his injury was the only reason she was around. "This is an assignment, nothing more. I'm doing Blue a favor."

She let that admission walk the room and relished the ray of hope that extinguished the moment he understood her meaning.

CHAPTER SIX

REIGN COULD FEEL HIM WATCHING AS SHE PUSHED MOST OF THAT DELICIOUS meal across the plate, since her appetite had waned because she was trying not to look at Devesh.

"You don't have to sit all the way over there," he said over the rim of his glass of sweet tea mixed with lemonade, snatching her out of her thoughts. "That chair looks so uncomfortable."

"It is," she said, leaving the dining room chair to take a seat on the chaise so she could stretch out and relax. "But it's fine."

"You can come closer," he challenged with a sly smile. "I don't bite unless you're into that sort of thing."

The lies you tell. She had no choice but to keep her distance. Touching him would only escalate things. She wouldn't dare fall for him all over again. She'd learned her lesson the hard way, and Devesh had made his choice. His traditional East Indian family over his love for her. Reign learned to live with that bitter pill, but couldn't recover her broken heart. She'd been foolish enough to believe they could make a go of it, anyway. Their May-December romance was doomed from the start.

"You're a pro, so how could you injure yourself at your favorite place?"

"I tried to keep the equipment from coming down on a woman who hadn't set it up properly," he answered, rubbing his thigh. "I caught it just in time, but in the wrong place."

"Or you could be honest and just say you were overdoing it."

"Not this time," he said, laughing at her true meaning that he gave too much time in the gym when he was already perfect. Her words, not his.

"I've seen some of those online workout videos of yours," she teased. "You're overdoing it. Even in those."

"Just showing people a few things they can do to keep in shape and build strength."

"No need to do all that," she said. "Even if you had a potbelly and extra weight, you would still look great."

Despite how humble he was, she wasn't far off the mark. Devesh seemed oblivious to the power he exuded simply by being himself. Towering height, olive complexion, a layered haircut that ended just at his shoulders. His muscular frame was the epitome of a man who took superb care of his body.

She couldn't believe some of the earlier pictures she'd seen of him as a scrawny little boy. He had such sad eyes, mostly because he, more than any of his siblings, had been bullied because of his accent. Plus, his ethnicity was different from the people of the area his family moved to when they came to America. The Bronx was nothing like East India.

Despite the odds, Devesh worked hard, focusing on finishing his education but also began a fitness regimen that transformed him. In time, he became a heartthrob and a rising Bollywood star. Only to have more established actors tear him down for his decision to personally research an upcoming role he had landed in a Bollywood movie. He had lived among the homeless and poverty-ridden masses to understand what they were experiencing. When competing actors posted pictures on social media and plastered his bedraggled image all over, it brought his acting career in India to a screeching halt. Perception was everything, and no one believed his reasons.

No one would hire him after that. No one wanted to be associated with poverty. It was cool to say that you're helping the homeless and the less fortunate, but to actually get in the trenches to understand? That had not been the right move to make. But how could he know how to help, unless he understood what help was needed? Throwing money at people only lasted so long. It was temporary. That experience was the main reason he had taken an interest in charities that help children.

"I'd look good with a gut and love handles?" Devesh said, roaring with laughter. "You're just saying that because you love me."

"Loved," she corrected in a lower voice. "Get it right—*loved*."

Devesh's smile vanished as fast as it had appeared. His expression grew somber and intense. "Loved?"

Reign leaned back onto the pillows on the chaise. "I expected too much from you. I mean, really. The age difference alone—"

"Can you stop saying that? You know it had nothing to do with that," he said, clearly annoyed with Reign's persistence.

"Oh, so your family was all right with the age thing?" she taunted, locking a steely gaze on him.

He grimaced as he stuttered, "Well … I … No, honey, it wasn't the age …"

"Sooooo," she crooned, stroking the honey gold skin on her left arm. "It's because of this right here."

Devesh winced, and his lack of response was its own answer. Reign gave him a smile.

"Yes, three strikes and I'm out. Age, color, and different cultures—Black and East Indian, and you thought we could do what? Have a life together? How were we supposed to pull that off? You're a Bollywood star that every mother from here to New Delhi is trying to lock into marriage. And I'm a sister from the Southside of Chicago, with a full-grown son and very little family to speak of. Yet, somehow you wanted a full life, children?" She shook her head. "I'm not having any more. Honey, my eggs are old enough to walk you down the aisle and marry you of their own accord."

"That's not funny," he countered, his lips pursed in stark disapproval.

"That's truth." She gave him a hard glare. "And it doesn't change the fact that you wanted more than I was willing to give."

"There are ways …"

"True, but not for us."

She turned up the television that showed a newscaster's report on the Ad Expo and some of the new products coming out in a few weeks. The camera panned to Devesh, who ignored the women who surrounded him trying to get a picture as he reached out to Reign when she walked past another one of the exhibits where he had been assigned.

Reign nodded toward the screen. "And you keep doing that, giving me all that attention, and those women who are indirectly responsible for your appearances are going to feel some kind of way and stop supporting you."

"I don't give a damn about them." He shifted on the bed. "They will not tell me who to love."

"Right, that's reserved for your family."

CHAPTER SEVEN

FAMILY WAS EVERYTHING TO HIM, BUT HE HAD REALIZED TOO LATE THAT they shouldn't be the only thing. The Shoreview Mansion in the northern area of California was the center of all the social activities for the Maharaj family. All the family, extended family, some of their friends and co-workers paid into a pot that purchased the groceries for dinners that were prepared for everyone on a nightly basis. Mumma, Aunts Kavya, Prisha, and Neerav kept everyone's babies, toddlers, and preschool-aged children during the day so that the women in the family could pursue their careers. The nightly dinners served as a haven to discuss many things or for everyone to pitch in to watch the children if a couple wanted to go out on a date or vacations.

When Devesh landed a major role in a Bollywood film, he had used every dime of that money to purchase that mansion in the warmer climate of California. Then he expanded it according to his Mumma and Papa's wishes. That was before moving the immediate family from New York to California—his parents Jasinder and Suresh, as well as his twin sister, Anaya, and her husband Pranav, his brother Bhavin, and wife Sana, sister Tiya, and her husband Hiran,

Soon, a host of aunts, uncles and cousins followed by settling in homes in nearby suburbs. There wasn't a time he could remember when his home wasn't filled with people laughing, celebrating, thriving, and experiencing a wonderful life here in America.

None of them were particularly pleased with his relationship with Reign. They thought it was a phase. They were wrong then. And given the way Devesh felt at the moment, they were wrong now.

"Reign, don't," he said, in a warning tone that matched his expression.

Duly chastised, she stood and smoothed the skirt down over her thighs. "My apologies, it seems like you're good here so," Blue should be here shortly. "I'm going back to my room."

"No …" he whispered, his voice halting her movements. "Honey, stay with me a little while longer." He lifted his leg and groaned in an overly dramatic fashion before placing it back on top of the stack of pillows on top of the paisley comforter. "I need you."

"You're milking this for all it's worth," she said, wagging a finger at him. "And don't think I don't know that you and Blue pulled a fast one to get me here."

A partial smile lifted the corners of his mouth as he tried to hide the truth, but the twinkle of mischief in his dark-brown eyes spoke volumes. "I don't know what you're talking about."

"The attendant's daughter's appendix burst?" Reign quirked an eyebrow, and raised her hands making air quotes. "When it was her turn to play doctor. Please."

Devesh gave her a sheepish grin, then outright chuckled. "Is that what Blue told you to get you here? I mean, I said any means necessary, but I didn't think she'd make up that big of a lie."

"Like I said, you're not slick."

"Can I help it if my circle of friends wants to give us a chance to reconcile?"

"What is there to reconcile?" she asked, exasperated by his single-mindedness. "Things ended before it even started. Family put on that heat, and you disappeared with no explanation." She shrugged and walked to the cathedral windows and looked out on the Atlanta skyline. "But that's all right. I've survived worse."

With her back to him, Reign looked down into the city, following the ant-like lines of traffic littering the highway below. "I'm serious about protecting my peace after a man told me something that shut me down. I didn't let anyone get close to me for years." She glanced over her shoulder and took in his questioning expression. "You changed all of that. Made me feel loved, made me feel wanted, made me feel beautiful again. And then …" She shook her head, folding her arms across her full breasts. "You know what? It doesn't matter anymore."

"It matters to me," he whispered. "What did that man say?"

Reign put her focus on the glimmering lights competing for sky space with the stars.

"What. Did. He. Say?"

CHAPTER EIGHT

REIGN WEIGHTED HOW MUCH TO SHARE WITHOUT OPENING ANOTHER wound. Shawn had showed up to her house that night three sheets to the wind and another five knots under the table. Unfortunately, he was sober enough to say something that made her world crumble. He believed that her self-esteem was so low that she would accept his new terms. He was wrong, during their sexual encounter that night Reign put a vaginal grip on his erection so tight that he experienced a painful muscle cramp that wouldn't go away no matter how much he stroked it. And he was working his hand as though he was trying out for the masturbation Olympics.

She watched him roll around on her freshly shampooed carpet, screaming in pain for an hour before the neighbors started banging on the wall and she finally called 9-1-1.

When two women paramedics rolled in to scoop him off her bedroom floor, take him down the stairs and into the waiting ambulance, Reign filled them in on what Shawn had said. Patty and Sandi—Reign would never forget their names—shared a speaking glance between them. They were also about Reign's size. Raven-haired Sandi said to her fellow blonde paramedic. "Looks like we'll be taking the *scenic* route."

Shawn came by two months later, begging for forgiveness and a second chance. Reign didn't allow him or any other man to touch her for years after that experience. She had already soured on relationships at fourteen after landing a lemon off the showroom floor. She didn't trust her instincts with men and eventually lost the need to be with one full time. Instead, she began experimenting with … toys. The I-Scream vibrator, The Cupcake, The Sword of Love—a dildo based on Doc Johnson's prize piece. She'd been a happy camper ever since. Until Devesh. Then she learned that she'd been missing out on the best part of what came with good sex. Correction—*great sex*, if she was honest when it came to Devesh. The kind that didn't originate from specially wrapped packages to hide the contents. The kind that wrapped their arms around you and pulled you close when they were done giving you several mind-altering orgasms. The kind that came from genuine connection and intimacy.

"He said, 'Black men don't really like fat women,'" she answered Devesh, trying to keep her voice from breaking at relaying those hurtful words. "'You'll have to pay me for sex from now on'."

Reign turned just in time to witness Devesh's anger flare, bringing a crimson hue to his olive complexion. He almost slid off the bed in haste to close the distance between them.

"What are you doing?" she squealed. "Stay off that leg. Let the salve and all that other stuff Blue gave you do its work."

"You know he was wrong, right?" he said, now situated in an awkward half on-half off position on the bed.

"That's not—"

She waved him back down.

"He was an asshole, pure and simple," Devesh chided, complying by settling into his space again, but still reaching for her. "And you let him into your head like that? He didn't deserve you."

"And what you did was any better?" she shot back, trying to keep her emotions in check because Devesh's abandonment was worse than what that man had said all those years ago.

"So, you deserve me now? A second chance? Should I have given *him* that second chance he asked for after I put him in the hospital?"

Devesh tilted his head. "Wait … what?"

"He had a ..." She tried and failed not to smile. "He had a cramp."

His eyebrow shot up as his gaze narrowed in on her. "Where?"

"Guess."

Devesh groaned and slid a protective hand toward the family jewels. "Ouch."

"Indeed, and the paramedics, who were plus-size women themselves, gave him a little hell of their own when I told them what he said." Reign let out a long, satisfying breath. "They took the scenic route to the hospital and conveniently forgot to give him any pain meds on the way. I carried that ugly rejection far longer than I should have. Until you came along to teach me another way to view life—and relationships."

Reign placed her hand against the cool glass of the window. The sunset image of the sun leaving and ushering in the night provide an amazing orange-blue hue dynamic. "It's so much safer not to do this love thing."

"You can't hold your love hostage for the rest of your life," Devesh warned. "That's not fair."

She remarked with a laugh as she whirled to face him. "What's that? There's nothing fair about anything that has to do with love. Here it is. A younger man made me feel so wonderful and then snatches it all away. What was that about?"

"I was immature," he protested and lifted off the bed a little, only to resettle again at her warning glare. "That wasn't on you."

"That may be true, but I was the one who should've known better. They couldn't see past my color."

Devesh scooted toward the edge of the bed. "I should've been stronger than that. I wasn't prepared for the anger and the arguments that came at me every single day, all day. I never heard enough of them."

He beckoned her to come closer, and she ignored him. "You're wrong about my family," he said. "We grew up here in America. My sister dated Latinos, Black men, Italian and—"

"Yes, but even she married an East Indian man when it came down to it, right?"

Devesh clamped down on whatever he was about to say, and she figured he had no comeback because she spoke the truth.

"She dated other races," Reign said, reclaiming her space on the chaise. She was closer, but still just out of reach. "But she *married* the exact way your family wanted. What makes you think it's going to be any different with you? The youngest male? And the only one in your family who has so much visibility in your culture." She crossed one leg over the other. "No sweetheart. You can play with me all day long, but in the end, your ass better bring home an East Indian woman of childbearing years. You know it, and so do I." She shrugged. "It's fine, though. Besides, I'm not holding my love hostage. I'm just not giving it to you. I have lots of love to share, but only with those who are deserving."

The silence between them was nearly as painful as not speaking to him, not seeing him for all this time.

"They will not run my life," Devesh said through clenched teeth. "I love you and that hasn't gone away. Seeing you here at the expo hit me so hard, then when you wouldn't even acknowledge me. My heart hurts just contemplating all the time we've lost; all the time we've wasted."

"We?" she shot back, then affected a thick accent. "What do you mean we, White man?"

Devesh shook his head at that familiar banter between The Lone Ranger and Tonto.

"I'm not White."

"Close enough when you're trying to put the blame on me for something that was all on you." Reign crossed her arms, satisfied she'd won this round.

He was silent so long she didn't think he would ever respond.

"You're right," he finally conceded. "It's time I owned what happened. My parents weren't going to approve, but instead of standing up for us. I panicked and put my family's wishes above my own … above yours." He sighed, and that sound was so full of regret. "The time I've wasted has tortured me. Nothing has been the same since we parted, and the most ironic thing is that you're the reason my career is on the rise."

CHAPTER NINE

DEVESH WAS RIGHT, BUT IT WASN'T BECAUSE SHE SET OUT TO DO SO. SHE simply hated that he was being dismissed without being given a chance. The East Indian culture deserved the same amount of representation as all others. Reign had made it a small mission of hers to ensure little Indian boys saw themselves in the media too. Devesh deserved the same chance that those Blue-eyed hunks were given.

When the members of the intellectual property firm she worked for walked the Vegas convention two years ago, Reign had witnessed the cruel way people treated someone who looked different from their normal model fare. But she suspected that the biggest issue was because Devesh commanded a room or space whenever he entered or walked past—a great deal of it was female attention. The companies and the competition were trying to figure him out. Native American? Italian? Latino? None came close to discerning his true ethnicity.

Reign was spurred into action when she saw that Devesh was being edged out for assignments by the blond, Blue-eyed, and green-eyed guys due to the common American standard of handsomeness.

She strode over to him and simply said, "I have an idea. Come with me."

Devesh didn't hesitate, though he had never laid eyes on her before. First, they took a trip to Moss Tailors who were able to put some things together for him. Then Devesh went up to his room and changed into one of the suits that draped his muscular frame to perfection. Next, she styled his hair to give it a layered look and took his electric razor, and put a little touch up and left that five o'clock shadow that women seem to love. Then Reign took a photo of him next to the cathedral windows of the lobby and a Vegas strip backdrop with him extending a glass of wine toward the camera. The shot was seductive and beckoned whoever was looking to join him. They went to the business office of the convention center, had several banners made with Devesh in different poses with a tagline of "Tall, dark and handsome is not a myth. It's a promise."

In an open space in the center of the main exhibits of the expo, Devesh set up that final vertical banner and stood next to it. Reign encouraged three women who were nearby to take a selfie with him and post it on their social media pages with the hashtag #talldarkandexotic. Soon, crowds of women were standing in line to take a picture with him as if he was a celebrity.

Some of the execs who'd dismissed Devesh earlier, watched the progression, and now wanted him to come to their booths to attract the consumers they were after. Devesh gestured to Reign and told them, "You need to speak to my lawyer."

"I'm not a lawyer," she protested where only he could hear.

"But you work for them," he responded, and his tone was absolute. "You'll know a good deal when you see it."

Right there, with women cheering him on, a bidding war ensued. They made off with six deals for Devesh to hold court at a different exhibit each day. That put nearly twenty grand in his pocket that week, as those who wanted to solidify his presence had to make instant transfers into his account to seal the deal.

"They could just invoice us."

"No, sir," she said with a patient shake of her head. "You are *not* chasing their money. Especially when they're chasing you. Take a lesson from the Queen of Soul. Aretha Franklin never began a concert without getting her cash *up front*. You never heard of her being in court trying to get someone to pay up. They knew the deal. Now these same people who gave you the side-eye at first, now understand how you work. You'd better get used to telling folks to roll you your coins."

Impressed, Devesh shelled out twenty percent to Reign via a currency app. When the notification of the amount showed up on Reign's phone. "I can't accept this. I merely stepped in to help you. What they were doing wasn't right."

"Your son is about to start a graphic design and printing business," he said. "Even if you can't seem to buy something nice for yourself, use it for him."

Later that night, they shared dinner and plenty of laughs over the responses and reactions of the other models, who were honestly jealous that the spotlight had shifted. Several even went so far as to play a few childish pranks involving Devesh's clothing and props. A few suddenly reconsidered and wanted to get close to Devesh, possibly trying to see what made him so fascinating to women.

After the expo, Devesh and Reign talked every day, sometimes three times a day, and texted just as much. The most unlikely friendship blossomed into an intimate relationship that neither of them expected. His family wouldn't hear of it.

Even his sister reached out to Reign at some point. "Ever since Devesh came back from Vegas, all he talks about is you." Her tone was serious and held a note of anxiousness. Anaya was Devesh's twin and, since she voiced concerns, it did not surprise Reign that Devesh's calls became less frequent. Soon, Devesh's older brother started working the modeling accounts, slowly replacing Reign as manager.

Eventually, Reign stopped hearing from Devesh altogether.

CHAPTER TEN

"I MISSED YOU. EVERY DAY," DEVESH CONFESSED, PULLING HER BACK TO the present. "You didn't view me as some pretty boy with no real plans in life. You saw the real me."

"That might be true and all, but it wasn't enough," she countered, struggling to keep the tears at bay. "I was fooling myself, thinking this thing between us could be something real."

Devesh shook his head. "No, you weren't, Reign."

"Hey, no worries," she said over the rim of her glass. "I'm a grown ass woman. Over the years, I have learned to cut my losses and realize when a situation is not meant to be."

Her gaze flicked over his face—the chiseled handsomeness of it, the lips that had a inviting sensual curve. But his eyes—those dark piercing eyes spoke to her in a way that penetrated her soul.

"This right here was beautiful, but it's just a fantasy," she told him. "To think it could last ... either you were lying to yourself, or I was. I needed more man than you could be at that time."

"At *that time*," he snapped, and a vein throbbed at his temple because she struck a nerve. "I've grown so much since then and I've realized what is most important. And I want you Reign King. No doubt about it."

Reign gave him a warning look, and he huffed and reclaimed his spot on the bed.

"My family can only do so much for me, but my woman is my everything." He beckoned for her, but she didn't comply, prompting him to say, "Come here."

"No, I'm good right here."

"Woman, don't make me hop after you."

Reign froze, then tried not to laugh at the classic line from an 80's comedy flick. She laughed and moved forward to settle next to him.

He held out his arms, inviting her into an embrace.

"Devesh, we can't do this."

"Just for a moment," he whispered. "Let me hold you so I can sleep and have sweet dreams."

She slipped off her heels, pulled her legs onto the bed, then inched a little closer, but kept a small space between them. "Have to be careful not to hurt your leg."

He lifted his eyebrow suggestively. "That's not the limb you need to worry about."

"Behave."

"What? Be *who*? Be *what*?" He looked over his shoulder as though someone was behind him, then shook his head in mock horror. "Be … whatever that was, I'm sorry that word does not exist in the Hindi language."

"You've got jokes," she said, chuckling.

He gathered her in his arms. "This is no laughing matter. I want you back in my life, Reign."

"But—"

"No excuses," he said, stroking an index finger down her cheek. "You still have feelings for me."

She slowly shook her head, unable to voice anything through the wave of emotions churning in her heart.

"Don't lie to me, woman." Devesh tightened his hold, and she placed her head on his massive chest. "Yes, I hurt you, and it wasn't right. I thought I could get over you. Nothing could fill that emptiness in my life after we parted—not work, not family, especially not the never-ending parade of boring, thirsty, or desperate single women all vying to become my wife."

Devesh pressed a kiss onto her forehead and a shiver of pleasure shimmied down her spine that triggered a delicious tingle in a few other places. "Reign, look at me."

"I need to go." She attempted to create some space between them. "I can't trust this. I can't trust you. I'm satisfied with my life the way it is. We can't—"

"The lies you tell."

She parted her lips to protest at the exact moment he leaned in to kiss her again. His tongue teased within until she softened and accepted his need for exploration. He was joy and pain. Sunshine and rain. A world of conflicting emotions in just one kiss—emotions that were welcomed and others so forbidden. He pulled his lips from hers just long enough to search her eyes, allowing a moment to truly make her wishes known.

"Reign, stay with me tonight," he said, stroking her back. "We'll work out everything when the morning comes, I promise. But tonight, I need you right here, in my arms."

She couldn't form a protest. Truthfully, it wasn't him she was worried about. She had fallen for him before because he had shown her more compassion, love, passion, and consideration than any other man had ever done in her life. He encouraged her to start the business with Blue and do something for herself besides being a mother and a woman who worked for a law firm. He challenged her ... *what is that you want to do that would bring you joy even if you didn't get paid for it*. Then he hit her with Jim Rohn's most famous quote: *If you work hard for yourself, you'll make a living. If you work hard on yourself, you'll make a fortune.*

His support was every shade of sexy. It would be so easy to get caught up in Devesh's spell again.

How could someone like him be attracted to a curvy woman with eyes that sometimes held the pain of her tragic upbringing before she settled into a regular, almost sedate kind of life in Chicago?

What did they truly have in common? Nothing but a love of being open and honest in communication, and thoughts of being happy and fulfilled. Devesh had shared his deepest desires with her and shown her passion beyond her wildest dreams, but good sex a marriage doesn't make. They never considered those things to be mutually inclusive.

Finally, he ended her confusion and silent misgivings by saying, "Go on, Reign. I'll call you if I need anything. I promise."

CHAPTER ELEVEN

PART OF HER HEAVED A SIGH OF RELIEF TO BE LET OFF THE HOOK, BUT another part of her was disappointed, too. She knew he wouldn't contact her if he needed help. The other people on Blue's list had already let her know how stubborn he had been. He tended to overexert himself and not take his injuries as seriously as he should. He had been ordered to stay off his feet for at least two weeks.

Devesh had a commitment to the companies that sponsored his appearance. Evidently, backing out at the last minute wasn't something he even considered. Especially with all that had been done for him to establish a foothold in the industry when his acting and career stalled.

She stood, undecided on what she should do, but then he made her halt when he said, "Tell me what happened since we lost touch."

This room was closing in on her. It held their pain and expectations. She had to get out of here.

"That's a longer conversation than we have time for," she said. "It's an amazing night, let's go for a walk."

"I'm not really supposed to be walking, remember?" Devesh said pointing to his swollen knee.

"I know that, but that doesn't mean I can't put you in a wheelchair and push you around. Let's go."

"I'm not getting in anyone's wheelchair," he said, shoulders tense. "No one has seen me in one since I've been here. I'd like to keep it that way."

"We need to let Blue's salve do its work." Reign walked over to the closet and pulled a t-shirt and a pair of shorts out of the closet, then tossed them at Devesh.

"Here put on your shirt and I'll help you with your shorts."

He looked at Reign, puzzled. "Where are we going?"

"What's wrong? Don't you trust me?" Reign gave him what was supposed to be a reassuring smile.

"I'd like to say yes, but I don't know how upset you are at me? I don't want to end up like that other guy."

Reign chuckled as she helped him slide into a pair of khaki shorts.

"Don't worry, if I was that angry with you. I would've taken care of you on day one. I guess I like you a little."

He gave her a side eye. "Okay, I trust you."

"Well then, let's go."

Reign helped Devesh get into the wheelchair flipped up the leg attachment so his knee was slightly elevated. She carefully placed an ice pack on his knee then pushed him towards the door.

"Wait, what about the guard?" he said, looking up at her over his shoulder.

"Don't worry about him. I've got a plan."

Reign navigated the wheelchair to the double doors of the suite, then peered out and found the guard stationed closer to another model's room. She then waited for the guard to make a sweep towards the other end, then pushed Devesh around the curve to the elevator and pressed the call button.

"Up?" he whispered. "I thought you said we were going outside."

"We *are* going outside," she whispered back. "We're going to the roof top."

"Ah, you were always the creative one."

"You betcha."

"Unless you're planning to throw me off," he said, narrowing his gaze on her.

"Tempting," she shot back and he stifled a chuckle.

Once Reign and Devesh were in the elevator and selected RT, they stood silently as a loud ping rang out in the small, enclosed space indicating their ascent to the roof top garden and second pool area of the hotel. Both of them were silently contemplating that kiss which served to reignite a flame that had never been quite snuffed out.

When they reached the top, they encountered a red-haired, freckled faced maître d' who asked if they had a reservation. He "somehow" found Reign's name on the list after she slipped him a crisp fifty-dollar bill. The waiter ushered them to a table on the patio overlooking the skyline. It was a clear night at a pleasant eighty degrees. Devesh inhaled savoring the night air.

"Now, isn't this better than being in that stuffy hotel room?"

"Yes, this is much better than being confined to that bed. The only reason I'd stay there is if you joined me."

Reign looked down at her smart watch and said, "Whew look at the time? Maybe we should've stayed in the room, I think your meds might be too strong."

"You know that I'm not on any medications," he said. "Now I'll ask you again, tell me what happened since we lost touch."

She closed her eyes for a moment and steadied her breathing. After moving her chair a little closer to Devesh, Reign filled him in on her life and some of the exciting cases she'd been a part of as a paralegal and becoming a partner in the business with Blue.

"Why do you call it The Native Lady?" he asked, when she spoke on the new business.

"I read a book, Navajo, about a guy who lives on a reservation in New Mexico. Darryl told us that his clan originated from one woman who was resilient and powerful. Her name is something I can't quite pronounce correctly, but the story is beautiful. We get some of our base elements from the Benally Farm."

Getting reacquainted led to a host of conversations, it felt like old times. Like they didn't have the world against them. They balanced each other like Yin and Yang. If one was missing, there was chaos. Devesh didn't want to admit it, but his new team of family didn't do nearly as good of a job as Reign had. Time slipped away from them and when Reign glanced at her smart watch it was midnight.

"Wow, its late, or rather early. The agency will kill me if you show up in the morning with bags under your eyes. "I'm going to take you downstairs and tuck you in, Mr. Maharaj." Then she checked her phone. "Blue hasn't even bothered to text or call. What the hell is going on with that woman?"

"Why don't you stay with me again tonight?" Devesh said. "It's not going to look good if you're tiptoeing to your room at this late hour."

"This is *not* summer camp, and we are *not* teenagers, Devesh. Besides it's no different from me tipping out of your room first thing in the morning," she countered, peeping his game.

His expression turned playful. "Well, at least people would think you got something out of it."

"That is *not* funny," she said, giving him a fiery glance.

"I assure you that when we arrive back to the room, you can remain on your side of the bed, and I'll remain on mine, and I'll do that ... um" he pretended to cough "... be ... um ... be ... ha" then he pretended to choke. "be ... *behave*."

She laughed as if she hadn't in a long time.

Reign stood and maneuvered him back to the elevator. They were both in good spirits from the calming night air.

The burly guard glared at them when they rolled down the hall leading to the suite. "Y'all are gonna get me fired."

"That's not going to happen," Reign said. "I've got people."

"Make sure those people can pay my bills," he countered looking over the rim of his glasses. "There are protocols in place for the models. Y'all could have asked for an escort and isn't that other woman supposed to be the night attendant?"

Reign parted her lips to speak.

"Won't happen again," Devesh said.

At the suite door, Devesh said, "I promise to behave," he said, putting up two fingers to signal he was giving scout's honor even though he'd never been a scout. "Besides, I can't do my best work if my leg isn't one hundred percent."

"But I thought that wasn't the leg I needed to worry about?" she said with mock innocence.

Devesh gave her a megawatt smile. "Touché."

CHAPTER TWELVE

After Reign got him settled back in the bed she settled on the chaise and picked up her book again, hoping that concentrating on the words would help keep her out of trouble.

"What are you reading?"

"Rebirth: Stepping Out of the Shadows and Into Your Own Light by Yvonne Elliott. It's a memoir -self-help kind of thing," she said, closing the book and pressing it close to her chest.

"Is there a need for a self-help book for a woman who's proficient in everything?" Devesh expressed, raising an eyebrow.

"If you must know, I don't have it all together, and this woman's story is amazing." She left her spot and handed it to him, and he flipped it over to read the blurb on the back cover. "She was only two and a half pounds at birth, and overcame her mother's drug abuse, her father going to federal prison, being shuffled from place to place, all before she was ten. Somehow, she still managed to achieve her goals."

Reign smiled as Devesh handed the book back and she said, "It's a reminder that if she can overcome adversity to accomplish her dreams, then so can I. That's why I took your advice and invested in The Native Lady with Blue." She sighed and traced the edges of the book. "You know a little of what I went through. I love a good rag to riches story. And even better when it's a woman I can relate to. I'm sure they have a few of those in India, too."

Devesh placed his head back on the pillows and focused on the textured semicircles on the ceiling. "You know, we have a myth about a young boy in India who grew up very poor. He came from nothing to end up on one of the most famous game shows in all of India. He won thousands of Rupees and went on to live an amazing life. He is my hero."

"Jamal Malik from the film Slum Dogg Millionaire is your hero," she said, squinting as she peered at him. "That's not a myth. You're such a bullshitter."

He burst into laughter at being busted—again.

"I should've known that wouldn't work on you," he said. "That movie is so antiquated that it has only influenced a few younger folks who have never seen it. I'm shocked that you have."

Reign smiled at Devesh, glad that he'd kept his spirits up despite the pain. He was not taking the easy way out when it came to his resolve not to take any opiates. So why had he done so when it came to their relationship? Was losing his family's love so important that he would give up so easily on their love? Could she believe him this time?

"I also seem to remember there being a woman in that movie, a woman who was just beyond reach," Devesh said. "They were like two ships passing in the night, but Jamil was determined to win her love." He locked gazes with her. "That's one thing I've learned about love is that when it's meant to be, the universe will conspire to make it happen."

He was talking more about their relationship, than the movie itself. Reign always loved to listen to Devesh reinterpret the books and movies he enjoyed. As much as she loved his words and the sound of his voice. there was no way she was going to fall for him again. Reign straightened up, remembering why she was there in the first place.

"Devesh, no matter how persistent you are, I won't fall for your charms this time. I already know what it feels like to play with fire and get burned. Fool me once, shame on me. Fool me twice..." Reign's voice trailed off as the hurt from their past rose to her throat. Reign reached down, taking a sip of her water to get her bearings.

Devesh could feel Reign's heartache even when she wasn't talking. Their connection was still so strong nothing could block it.

"Reign, my only regret was not standing up for you when I had the chance. I was a coward and there's no other way to explain it."

Before Devesh could finish his sentence. Reign's reminder went off, stopping him from saying anything more.

"Ah, Ah. No time for talking, it's time for you to take some of the natural supplement to help with the inflammation." Reign put the book aside, went back to the fridge and took out some orange juice, and a small container of leftovers from Paschals. As Reign prepared a tray her mind wandered back to a time before all of his family drama, a time when her heart ached for him. They hadn't been in the same space for so long she forgot how strong their attraction really was.

Reign went back to Devesh's bed, carrying the tray of his snack.

"Here you go. Your supplements are on the left. I reheated everything else. Eat up and you'll be sleeping in no time," Reign said.

The sooner you fall asleep, the sooner I can go back to my room. She didn't want to admit it, but spending this much time alone with Devesh made her nervous and he probably could tell.

"You keep feeding me like this and I won't be able to fit into anything I brought with me. You always know just how to take care of me. Just like the wife my mother always wanted for me."

"Yeah, a wife that's just in the wrong body and skin," Reign said with a tone as sharp as a Ginsu knife.

"My parents will adjust." Devesh leveled an intense gaze on her.

"Really? But what about everyone else? Do you really think I could take being a second-class citizen with my husband's own family for the remainder of my life? I don't need it at home, I get enough of it every single day in those streets," Reign said pointing towards the hotel window.

Devesh slammed his spoon down on the tray. "Damn it, Reign!"

He rarely cursed, so that immediately made her sit up and take notice.

"What can I do to make you understand that I've learned my lesson. Losing someone so valuable can make you do that. I'd go to the ends of the earth for you. I'd leave them, if it meant I'd get to spend the rest of my life waking up to you. Damn," Devesh growled, wincing.

Reign came closer to him, moving the tray out of the way. Here, let me look at that."

"No, it's fine," he said, grimacing.

"Let me look," she commanded, pulling back the covers to inspect the damage. Reign's gaze traveled up his legs, surveying the black dry fit compression shorts that concealed the gift bestowed upon him by God. She glanced down again, his right knee had clearly swollen twice the size of the left. The makeshift icepack would work a lot better if he'd behave. *Oh, but he doesn't know that word.*

"Well, here's our problem right here," she said. "Your ice pack has gone from frozen to cold water. I'll get some more ice, then I'll rub you down with Blue's concoction. She said it has oils and herbs from India that should make everything feel all better."

"Are we talking about the *right* leg again?" Devesh replied, grinning.

"I'm not going there with you," she said, chuckling when he winked. "Not tonight."

CHAPTER THIRTEEN

Laughing along with her, he watched as Regin moved around the suite, being the perfect nurse. From the moment she invested time in him to shine above the men who had belittled and taunted him, she had made sure all of his needs were met. Made sure the contracts were right, that the company took care of his lodging, meals, and transportation and he had front and center in all advertising campaigns. Her caring nature had melted his frustrations and made him love her even more.

Why had he let his family take that away from him? They could not replace what he had with Reign. Most of his siblings had a mate, even had children already. He was the only one who had not found "the one". Until he had. Then he let her slip away.

"Okay, here we go," Reign said, returning with a fresh ice pack in one hand and a small jar in the other.

"What is that in the jar?" he said, inching back. "You know I don't do drugs. I've seen what they can do to people. I'm not so ego-driven to believe that it can't happen to me."

Reign unscrewed the cap and took a whiff of the mysterious mixture, then placed it under his nose.

"You know Blue would never give you anything to hurt you. This is a stronger salve should have you up and about in no time. You'll be smelling like a bunch of old grandads, but it'll have you as right as rain."

"Right as ... *Reign*? I like the sound of that."

She shook her head at his play on words, then placed the items on the nightstand, before pulling the blanket to his feet. When she attempted to put the salve on her hands Devesh stopped her.

"Wait, take off your shawl," he said. "I don't want you to get anything on your clothes."

Reign smirked and slid the shawl from her shoulders and placed it on the edge of the bed. Then she rushed into the bathroom and grabbed a towel to place on the stack of pillows that elevated his legs and washed her hands.

"Let me know if anything hurts," Reign said as she slowly rubbed the strong-smelling oil-based cream above Devesh's swollen knee and down his leg.

"Just my heart, because it's missing you."

"You know what?" Reign said playfully smacking his arm. "Just relax, lover boy."

At first, he was tense as Regin placed her hands on him, but he soon melted into her touch. The supplements, her hands and the salve's heat lifted his mood.

"Ahh," Devesh sighed, allowing his body to sink in the pillows.

"See, there you go. Just calm down," she coaxed. "I've got you. Pain sends signals from the knee and leg to the brain. It's not enough to have your knee and leg relax; your mind has to as well."

Reign continued rubbing until the thick white mixture disappeared into Devesh's skin. After a few minutes, Reign put more salve onto her hands and moved to Devesh's other leg.

"What are you doing? We're being good remember," Devesh said playfully.

"Calm down, I'm not getting fresh with you. I know there's nothing wrong with the other side, but I think it's getting jealous."

"I think you just want to put your hands on me," Devesh whispered in his relaxed state. The mixture Blue had created was pushing him into a relaxed state of mind.

Reign finished the massage put the ice pack on his knee, pulled the comforter up, then tiptoed around the room cleaning everything up.

She wanted to make sure the next attendant would be good to go when they arrived in the morning. Today, she was going to hunt Blue down and figure out what was going on with her friend. It was totally unlike her to disappear like this. And this didn't feel like a set up at all.

As Reign was gathering her things to leave, Devesh whispered. "Don't start something you don't want to finish, it's not fair to tease me."

"If I was teasing you, we wouldn't be talking right now," Reign shot back from her place near the door.

"Reign, please stay," he whispered. "Just for one more night."

The husky promise in his voice was everything.

"Devesh, I …" Reign started. Her resolve was weakening and Lord knows she'd missed sleeping next to a warm body. But she also knew she had to stay strong.

"It's not like I can do my best work when I'm laid up like this and smelling like I bathed in Ben Gay, Aspercreme, and Icy Hot all in one. I mean, that's one hell of a sexy combination, right?"

"It doesn't smell that bad. It's all natural herbs, and she put some Lavendar in it to mask the stronger stuff." She inhaled the scent on her hand. "It's actually kind of a turn on."

Devesh patted the space next to him. "Just rest with me, honey."

Reign's gaze locked onto Devesh's and for a few moments her heart melted. Those dark brown eyes intent and mesmerizing. "All right, I'll stay," she said with a weary sigh.

Her body ached for him but as much as she wanted to be with him in a more intimate way. She knew the dangers involved, but he was also right about something else—Blue's mixture was practically causing her eyes to water.

Reign went into the bathroom for a few minutes.

When the bathroom door shut, Devesh did a quick scent check of his breath and underarms, slid off his shirt and took some water from his glass and sprinkled it on his hair. Reign walked back in just as Devesh was checking himself out on his phone.

She froze mid step. "What are you doing?"

"Just making sure I look my best."

"Why? You're about to take your ass to sleep, there's no need for 'best'."

"Just because I'm aching doesn't mean that I can't look good."

Hmmm, you don't have to do much. But that's clearly a bunch of bull.

Reign moved past the glass table to the side of the bed and perched on the edge, her back to Devesh.

"Are you nervous?"

She shrugged. "I've slept with a man in the same bed before."

"Right because your poly … poly … What is it again?"

"Polyamorous, Devesh, you know what that is. I believe that monogamy is an outdated relationship model."

His jaw tightened as he gave that some thought.

"What's wrong?"

"If you were my woman—my *wife*, I'd never want another man, woman or couple to be intimate with you."

"That's where you get it wrong," she said while avoiding eye contact. "Poly is not just about sex, it's the ability to love more than one person. Unlike you, I should be able to open my heart to another man and allow him to love me without having to lose a piece of myself. See, if I had been with someone else when you decided to kick me the curb." He grimaced. "It wouldn't have hurt so much. All I had was you. I never want to make that mistake again. Core memory locked and loaded."

Devesh's gaze narrowed to slits and his jaw clenched. She'd hit a major nerve with that one.

"I waded in monogamous waters for a long time and almost lost myself. One thing that I'm clear on, is that having a man, and a plan is the way I'd go the next time around."

Reign slid the shawl from her shoulders. Devesh watched the soft garment fall to the floor and Reign's silky skin floated softly on the starched white pillow.

Somehow, he didn't have a comeback for what she'd said. So he played it safe and remained silent.

"Comfortable?"

"A little, just keep your hands to yourself," she warned. "This isn't a booty call, I might be poly, but I know where my parts are, you know where your parts are. Neither the twain shall meet."

Devesh's deep smooth laughter filled the suite. "I never said we were having sex, did I?" He countered. "The last thing I need is for you to take me for any other man. When the time is right for us to indulge in making love, Kamadeva the goddess of love, will guide us to one another."

Devesh crossed his arms in a matter-of-fact manner and tried to blink away the signs of frustration.

"Are you trying to convince me with that line, or yourself?" Reign remarked, giving him a half-smile.

Devesh lowered his arms and propped up on one elbow.

"You've only experienced ten percent of the love that I have for you. You'll grasp the depth of my love once we get married.

Devesh decided he'd had enough of these games with Reign he needed to show her deep down how much he loved her and wanted it to be a forever kind of thing.

"Married? We can't even get to the seriously dating stage."

He stroked his fingers across her arm, causing a tingle to ripple through her. "I know it'll take some time for you to believe me, and I intend on spending the rest of my life showing my love for you, and to anyone who will listen." He placed his hand on her shoulder giving it a squeeze and said, "Why is there so much tightness here?"

"I was supposed to be relaxing and have a staycation. No more volleyball this week. I had several books lined up to read, but then Blue penciled herself into my staycation twice. First for me to come to Atlanta to take over the process with the manufacturers. Then I received a second call saying she had a friend who would not behave…"

He smirked and said, "I don't have any idea of what you speak."

"So here we are," she said with a shrug. "Two birds and all that."

"I always hated that saying," he mused, scratching his head. "Why would anyone want to kill a bird."

"It's a figure of speech, sort of like the early bird gets the worm."

"Yes, but the worm was early too, and look what happened."

CHAPTER FOURTEEN

"I CANNOT PLAY WITH YOU," SHE SAID, EXHALING. "I'M GOING TO GET ONE of those thirty-minute massages at the expo later today. The booths in the health and wellness section have all kinds of health products, but there's one booth that's pulling in people with those minute massages. The line almost reached outside the convention center."

Devesh pondered that for a moment. "I can do that. Let me give you a massage to show you how I appreciate you for tending to my needs this weekend," he said. "Especially since Blue had to beg you to come in the first place."

"You don't have to do that but ... I could use a massage," Reign said suddenly feeling the tightness of her thighs from the last volleyball match. She was a killer from the serving line, but she also wasn't the youngest player there and that reminder sometimes came the day after with a few aches.

"All right," Devesh said. "One massage coming up."

"You know what? I'll think I'll wait for the expo." She inched backward. "You don't know the meaning of that *one* word."

Devesh released a low, throaty chuckle. "It's a safe bet that my leg will keep me from getting into any trouble."

"Men have done more with less." Reign got up from the bed, went to the closet and slid one of his shirts from a hanger, then went to the bathroom all while silently reciting the Lord's prayer in her mind.

She shut the door. Once inside she looked at the reflection in the mirror. *Reign, girl what the hell are you doing?*

As bad as she wanted to feel Devesh's muscular hands against her bare backside, a small part of her knew she had to resist. She wasn't just playing with fire. She sensed the heat in more places than one. A little of him could be dangerous. She held onto her last threads of strength, guarding a vulnerable part of her heart, body and soul.

She slid into the shower and let the water flow over her body before lathering.

Lead us not into temptation … because I have already found it myself.

Maybe accepting Blue's request was a sign it was meant to happen. She could've said no. A flat out no. But she wanted to be with him as much as it seemed that he wanted to be with her. Devesh was that forbidden love that came oh so close but stayed out of reach.

Reign stepped over the threshold dressed in just his shirt and not much else, to find a few dimly lit candles placed around the room. Rose petals leading from the bathroom door to the bed. She inhaled frankincense and vanilla, their two favorite scents. *Damn, was I gone that long?*

"Well, well someone's feeling *much* better."

"It was the supplements, Blue's salve and your massage," he said a little too smoothly and with an innocent look that she knew for an absolute ruse.

Chocolates—her weakness—were on the nightstand, along with a purple cymbidium orchid. A Woodson Collection journal with a woman on the cover with the words *resurrect her*. He remembered all of the little things. She was going to strangle Blue when she laid eyes on her. Wait a minute, this had more of Jay's touch to it. She couldn't strangle her son, but maybe she'd threaten to spank him again.

"I see, well I'll have to have Blue send a king-sized jar home with you."

Reign lowered his shirt from her shoulders and laid on her back looking up at Devesh. He didn't bother to speak for a moment, just looked at her with such longing it took her breath away.

"I."

"Shhh," he said placing his fingertip to her lips. "Let me take care of you."

Devesh limped over to the glass coffee table. She wanted to chastise him that he was doing way too much. Then his thighs flexed through the soft material as he bent over to retrieve a hunter green satin sash from the table. He maneuvered to the head of the bed and stretched his arms, extending a wide piece of fabric her way.

"Sit up for a moment," he said, with a low tone beckoning her to comply. "I just want you to concentrate on my voice."

Reign hesitated a moment but finally did as he asked. None of this had anything to do with a massage. Devesh tied the fabric over her eyes while lowering her back down onto the bed. "Poly my ass," he said against her ear. "You're mine, honey, and I'm going to make you forget any thought to the contrary."

Devesh serenaded her with a soul-stirring rendition of The Isley Brother's *You're All I Need*. His deep voice was nothing short of mesmerizing and she allowed the words to flow through her mind.

Reign's breathing became scarce in anticipation of whatever Devesh had planned. He picked up a familiar-looking bottle of warm oil from the bedside and massaged Reign's shoulders. It only took a few strokes for him to sense how tense and nervous she felt. He gazed at her a while, then put special attention on areas that felt more tense than others. The scent of this mixture wasn't anything like the salve that Blue had given to Reign.

Even though Reign was sharpened by her workplace position and education. At work, she was the boss, the work wife—whatever the firm needed. But here, in this space at this moment, Devesh was the one in charge. She loved it. They discovered it was her place of solace, the one place where she didn't have to know the answers or solve the problems. The moment she entered this part of his world, she was at his mercy, she didn't have to think. She could truly let go.

Devesh massaged her coated skin, wanting to take his time savoring every part of her body. They had been away from each other for far too long. He stroked her ever so slowly, committing every inch of her skin to memory.

Reign reveled in that passionate torment as her body moved like soft waves against the warm sands of a sun kissed beach. She was practically putty in his arms, but he wanted more. His goal was to prove that he was the one for her and he would—and could—please her in every way. Maybe then she could truly move past what his family had done to tear them apart. Maybe then she would know that she could trust him with her heart—again.

"Time to roll over, my love," Devesh said removing the blindfold.

"So soon?" Reign complied and was on her stomach while propping her hands under her chin.

"Don't worry, we have all night," he said. "Keep your hands right there. Don't move them. Honey, in this moment, do you trust me?"

She thought about what he really meant. In this moment, just the two of them. No outside world or influences. *Did she trust him?*

CHAPTER FIFTEEN

"Yes," she answered in a breathy whisper.

"Yes, *what*?" he shot back in a tone that was much sterner. "I need you to speak in full sentences."

"Yes, Devesh in this moment. I trust you."

With that being said, the tense air in the room dissipated.

"Good, for the good of all and the harm of none. I submit myself to you. I promise I will never hurt you again for as long as we both shall live."

A shiver of pleasure ran up Reign's spine. His tone was so matter of fact as if he were reciting his morning prayers. Reign's submission stirred something inside of him. As much as it looked like she was all business, behind closed doors he was well aware of what she needed.

No one else could connect to Reign like he could.

Devesh selected the next item from the table. The soft leather strap was Reign's favorite and Devesh was an expert at applying the right amount of pleasure and pain. He dragged the heavy leather tendril down Reign's legs as she arched her back trying to anticipate the next move.

Thwap!

Soft enough that it didn't hurt too much, but hard enough for her to know he meant business.

Reign gasped as she felt heat emanate from her right thigh. She then blew out a slow breath focusing on the cool air blowing on her naked body from his lips soothing the area and creating another sensation entirely.

Thwap!

"Aaaaahhhh," she moaned with the matching sting on her left ass cheek.

As she finished that exhalation, it was followed by soft touch of Devesh's lips and ice against her newly created sensitive spot. He took care kissing every inch, reminding Reign of his admiration and respect for her.

After paying careful attention to Reign's sites of awakening. Devesh grabbed the heavy leather strap and once more laid a strong swipe across her backside. Reign's moans filled the suite. They were just the right indicator of receiving pleasure and pain as she worked to catch her breath as her thighs stung. Devesh placed his hand lightly around the back of Reign's neck, giving it a soft squeeze as he pulled her to him. Never had she felt so safe and secure as being contained in his firm grasp. Devesh kissed her neck before loosening his grip.

"I thought you said Kamdevah would tell you when the time was right?" Reign said in a soft tone.

"Oh, she told me during my morning prayers, that today was the day. And what Kamdevah has put together, let no man put asunder."

Reign exhaled softly, releasing the last of her worries from her body and mind. No one existed in their world except them and the sensations. Devesh kissed Reign softly on the soft swell of her buttocks and whispered into her ear. "My Good Girl. Are you ready to receive?"

"Yes."

"Yes, *what*?"

"Yes, I am ready to receive."

This type of banter was their norm. They discovered early on in their relationship that they had a mild interest in BDSM—a variety of often erotic practices or roleplaying involving bondage, discipline, dominance and submission, sadomasochism. Together, they traveled down that rabbit hole of learning more about each other.

Reign further settled into her makeshift bondage position fluttering her eyes, her body tingling with anticipation as she waited for Devesh's next move.

"Don't ruin the mood by reinjuring your knee," she warned, noticing that not once had he winced or flinched with any pain for the efforts he had taken. Those endorphins must have kicked in, or Blue's potion ... must truly be magic.

"I'll worry about me. You just make sure you don't move your hands."

Devesh's next steps created a core memory so engrained in Reign's brain that she would remember what happened long after her right mind disappeared. He started his exploration by kissing the dimples at the small of Reign's back then slowly draped his tongue along the mountainous rise of her backside.

Reign's senses went wild as whimpers of pleasure escaped her lips and increased to moans. He teased one of her most secret erogenous zone. Her breathing became shallow, before she reached her first climax of the night.

Devesh knew all the right ways to make Regin ... rain. He placed his hands on her thighs stroking with a rhythm that allowed her heart and mind to relax again.

He tossed the strap on the floor as he tried to hold back, but his desires had reached that ultimate level. He had missed her so much. He had missed this so much. Patience got the best of him as his prepared to feel her become closer to him than he'd ever been before. This was more than just making love. He was preparing to take her mind.

"You smell so sweet, honey. I'm going to enjoy showing you just how deep my love goes. Tell me that you're ready for me."

She hesitated a few moments and his intense look encouraged her to whisper, "I am ready for you." Her request was thick and lingering as she uttered the words.

Devesh carefully placed his hands on Reign's thighs before sliding them up her voluptuous hips. Then he flipped her back onto her back, took his time and moved her to the center of the bed then patiently maneuvered her legs and arms until they extended towards the four corners of the bed. Her limbs were outstretched onto the king-size mattress, exposed like a sacrifice to the goddess of lust.

Once Reign was in the position that Devesh wanted, he moved until his face was level with those full sultry breasts and paused to run his tongue across his lips before his lips enclosed around the taught nipple that greeted him like a long-lost lover. Her moans were a symphony as he worked south tasting her soft skin and the curves of her body.

Reign looked down as Devesh positioned between her thighs and watched as his tongue danced along those intricate folds, stopping when he reached her new flower adornment. His head tilted slightly to the side, questioning the unique color choice of the tattoo, recognizing it as his favorite. His gaze meet her dark eyes looking down at him. A smirk crossed her lips.

Reign winked at him displaying her bratty side while still giving him hints of submission. She knew exactly what she was doing. The voiceless, but playful banter that passed between them like a tennis match gave her a source of gratification. She could sense that she could push Devesh too and enjoyed imagining creative ways to make him yield to her every whim.

He took a moment to stare at the lotus, a flower that rises from the mud without standing, and returns to the murky water each evening and opens their blooms at the break of day. Lotus are symbols of strength, resilience, and … *rebirth*. "We'll talk about this later, but for now I've got work to do."

Devesh carefully angled until he was hovering over Reign. Not one ounce of pain, flickering on his face.

"Are you ready for me to devour you?" he asked as a tear streamed down Reign's face and the low vibration of his voice danced through her ear drums.

"I've been ready since the moment I stepped into the room."

CHAPTER SIXTEEN

DEVESH'S FINGERS TRACED ALONG HER WET FOLDS OFFERING HIM THAT sensual nectar it was like Sunday communion, something to wash away the sins of the past. Then his muscular arms lifted Reign's legs onto his shoulders bringing her wetness to his face Devesh stuck out his tongue teasing against her folds, parting then, tasting her as if she was the best ice cream on earth.

Reign closed her eyes tightly, concentrating on the feeling of his soft tongue against that special place where sunsets went to rest, and moonlight came to life. No man had ever given her this much attention. Just as Reign thought she would cross over to the other side, where little deaths occurred and resurrection happened right after. She was very close to the edge. He was playing with fire and knew exactly how to stoke the flame.

Devesh removed his mouth from her mound, lowered her hips down on the bed then took his fingers and dipped them once again into that sweet nectar then pressed his fingers a few inches in, putting pressure on the spongy circle of nerves within Reign's front wall, stimulating it to the point that her eyes closed and her head went back, and she arched towards him. Her body trembled uncontrollably to the point he gripped her to hold her steady.

"Did you just release without permission?"

Her eyes flew open and locked on him, mortified that she had committed a cardinal sin. She averted her gaze and her uneven breathing made him smile inwardly because control and submission warred within.

Devesh placed his hands on the small swell of her back and commanded, "Close your eyes."

She complied immediately. All Reign could do was experience the heat emanating from Devesh's body, the mix of pheromones, along with the scented oils that accompanied every inhale.

"You'd better not climax again without my permission. Do you understand?"

She clenched her thighs around him as she gasped with the whisper soft touched on her pearl that nearly made her scream again.

"Yes, Sir. I understand."

"Open your eyes," he commanded.

"I want to see the fire in your eyes as I enter you. I need to see into your soul," Devesh said as he adjusted, favoring the right side, preparing to enter the moist heat of her. Reign's thighs instinctually wrapped around him as he looked deep into her eyes as he entered inch by torturous inch. His hands gripped her round buttocks and the softness made him inhale, and then he thrust in one fluid motion, and buried his face in her breasts. Those tight inner walls spread for him as though *they* were happy he was home.

Devesh pulled her into him then let her sink again as though he was doing a series of sets at the gym. A deep growl escaped him as her nails dug into his back. Her face rested at the nape of his neck as she released soft purring breaths. His desire to have her as close to him as possible caused him to bounce a little too hard forcing Reign to stifle her screams on Devesh's shoulder. That move was so hard it caused her teeth to graze his skin. Reign did as she was told, being careful not to leave any marks on his neck.

As much as he didn't care, the last thing she needed was for his nosey family to question what he had done when he met them for breakfast in the morning.

She concentrated on pulling those walls around him, holding him inside, milking him like he was the last source of sustenance on earth. Devesh continued his slow deliberate strokes as her motions matched his. Her moans echoed off the walls louder signaling to Devesh's that she was close to her second peak of the night.

Through short breaths Reign pleaded, "Sir, may I please cum?

He thrust in again and she gasped, "Not yet. Noooooo. Not yet."

Another thrust and she gripped his buttocks hard as her body tensed, trying to keep that orgasm at bay. She whimpered with the effort it took to maintain control and he could sense she was being torn apart.

"Yes, honey, you may cum."

Reign trembled as she exhaled and the pleasure whipped through her. The warm wet tightness around him rendered him powerless. He flexed, trying to prolong the pleasure just a little longer. His body betrayed that effort to hold back, and he groaned as his seed spilled deep into Reign's womb.

CHAPTER SEVENTEEN

THE MORNING SUN RAYS WERE SHINING THROUGH THE SHEER CURTAINS causing Reign to squint as she tried to open her eyes. Her body ached in places she forgot even existed.

After they showered, they had fallen asleep in each other's arms after that amazing night of passion.

Reign didn't know what cruel trick the universe was playing on her to make her fall head over heels in love for a man she could never have but she certainly didn't like it. Her mother abandoned her the minute Reign put her hypocrisy on blast in front of the church. Her father abandoned her because he simply didn't want the responsibility anymore. The rest of her family, besides Jay, had abandoned her when she told the police why her uncle had killed her sister. Roberto abandoned her because he blamed her for getting pregnant. Shawn came along after that causing devastation by rejecting her because of her size. Devesh had abandoned her because of his family who rejected her because of her age and ethnic background.

She looked over at Devesh's messy hair strewn across his face as he silently slept, admiring his chiseled features and smooth skin.

Reign made a mental note of Devesh breaking her heart last time and how it was nearly her undoing. There was a pattern she couldn't seem to break. And she wanted someone to choose her this time. As much as he loved her, and last night was the best it had ever been, Devesh still wasn't ready.

Core memory locked. You love him, but he loves his family more. Protect your heart at all costs.

She moved, attempting to extract herself from his hold and he tightened his grip. She had no choice but to stay put. Reign closed her eyes and turned her head into his chest.

They were startled by a knock on the door.

"Damn," Reign said, waking up with a start.

"Morning, honey," Devesh said, stretching languidly.

She scrambled off the bed, grabbed her clothes, then nearly stumbled as she made a mad dash for the bathroom and peered out through a crack in the door.

Devesh wrapped a towel around his waist and hobbled towards the door with a much better gait than he'd had all week. "Just a minute."

His pace gave Reign just enough time to slide into her clothes, then hop back into the chair at the far side of the bed. She smoothed her hair, slid into her shoes, trying to act like she had been in the chair all along.

Devesh chuckled and titled his head. She nodded.

"Good morning, Mr. Devesh," the daytime attendant said in a voice that was much too cheery for this time of day. Reign was definitely a night person.

"Good morning, Jerrod. How are you?" Devesh said as if he hadn't been putting in the Lord's good work that night and giving her a mind-blowing sensual experience.

"I'm amazing. I'm here to take you to your physical therapy appointment."

"That's great. I need to shower and get dressed. Could you give me a minute. And I think I can handle that on my own."

Reign wondered how Devesh could be so calm. Just looking at him made her insides tingle.

"Oh, this is my night attendant Reign," Devesh said in a formal tone.

Jerrod's gaze shifted to her and he gave her a onceover and a smile. "Hello Ms. Reign, is it Miss, Mrs. or Ms.? I want to make sure I have the salutations right, it's so important these days."

"It's Ms. but my last name isn't Reign."

"It is okay, Sugar. I'm a Southern boy and my momma taught me to start things off right. so I'll call you Ms. Reign." Jerrod sharply turned around towards Devesh. "Well, let's get a move on sir. Time is someone else's money."

"Not your money?" Devesh asked.

"My money is never tied up in someone else's time."

"I hear you, Devesh said on the way to the bathroom.

As Devesh made his way to the chair, Reign grabbed his shave kit that contained his medicine and the salve.

"Don't forget this, I wouldn't want you to be in pain while you're out," Reign said, and he cracked the door to accept the bag.

She looked into Devesh's eyes waiting to see something.

"Y'all don't have to act on my account," Jerrod said. "If y'all need a few moments, I'm good to come back."

Devesh stepped over the threshold and looked at Jerrod at the same time Reign put her gaze on him too.

"I don't know what you're talking about," Devesh protested.

"Stevie Wonder, Ray Charles, and Hellen Keller can see y'all are in love." He shrugged then crossed to the door leading to the hallway and lowered his voice as he said, "I'll come back in thirty minutes." He left before they could say anything else.

Devesh took a look at her horrified expression and asked, "Want to join me in the shower?" He gave a suggestive lift of his eyebrow.

"Absolutely not, I'm going upstairs and get changed."

"Can't trust yourself not to keep your hands off me." Then he kissed her to keep in whatever smart remark she had planned.

"Reign?"

"You're going to be late, Devesh."

"Will you be here when I come out?"

Reign struggled with giving him her most winning smile and he kissed her again, and she put as much of what she felt for him with every touch of their lips.

"I want you," he whispered, placing a kiss on her forehead. "That's all that matters."

Devesh made his way to the bathroom with a little more pep in his step. Evidently, he wouldn't be using a wheelchair today.

The moment that bathroom door closed, she stood in the center of the bedroom and couldn't stop replaying last night in her mind. He was belting out a pretty good rendition of the Shalimar's *Make This a Night to Remember*.

She could still inhale the scent of Devesh's oils on her body and hated that she'd have to wash them away. But then again, they could always put on more … later.

I love him. Core memory locked. *And shower sex is always amazing.*

Reign couldn't help but laugh as she undressed and joined him in the shower.

REIGN AND DEVESH CONTINUES IN LOVING ME FOR ME

Reign had never forgotten her whirlwind romance with Devesh, a Bollywood superstar. But their fiery passion and relationship ended abruptly due to their different cultural backgrounds and her own heartbreaking secrets. Now, five years later, she's a successful businesswoman with a secret that is still struggling to trust men.

When a chance encounter reunites her with Devesh, she's both thrilled and afraid. Devesh is now a wealthy international model and determined to be with Reign despite his family's disapproval. As they try to navigate their rocky relationship, old wounds resurface, including those from Reign's reckless exes and Devesh's traditional family.

Devesh is determined to protect the woman he loves and will do whatever it takes, even if it means taking down those who stand in their way. As their love is put to the ultimate test, Reign and Devesh must confront their deepest fears and decide if their love is worth fighting for. *Loving Me for Me* is a steamy and emotional journey of love, trust, and sacrifice that will leave you breathless.

Read to find out more or download your copy today
https://books2read.com/Lovingmeforme

"MY GOD THEY LOOK LIKE US."

Reign's heart took a quantum leap into her throat. The deep timbre of that voice belonged to the one man she never wanted to lay eyes on again. Before she could catch up to the hostess and make it to the nearest exit instead of the reserved table, he spoke again.

"Reign?" Her name carried across Tiffin Restaurant, causing a few heads to turn in his direction.

She nodded slowly, unable to get her vocal cords to produce any sound.

Devesh rose from the table where a group dressed in vibrant East Indian garments had gathered, and sauntered along the path to Reign and the two children he, up to this point, knew nothing about.

One night with him a little more than five years ago had changed her life. Reign had left her soul in that luxury hotel room and walked away with a broken heart—and a pregnancy—neither of which any woman with a grown son would have ever desired.

She had blocked all communication with Devesh that next day and made it her business to stop traveling in circles where they would come in close contact. She had managed to avoid him for so long; yet, a trip with the twins to Disneyland had placed them directly in his path.

Her children, Leena and Kamran, were unaware of the turmoil warring within her. They released their hold on her hands and ran to Devesh, offering an embrace. Though Reign had kept knowledge of their existence from Devesh, she'd made sure Leena and Kamran knew about him. For some reason, they'd been asking about him more and more lately. She showed them current images of him so that in the case of her untimely or accidental death, they would know exactly who their father was. She had even braced herself for the possibility that they might seek him out when they became teenagers if not before. She certainly wasn't prepared for a chance meeting like this. How could fate be so cruel?

Devesh lowered to his knees so he was at their eye level before glancing over Leena's shoulder as he asked, "Are these your children?"

Reign nodded, her voice still failing. She'd never imagined seeing her twins with Devesh, but in this moment, their resemblance to him was nothing short of astounding. Leena and Kamran carried Devesh's olive skin, raven hair, well-defined cheekbones—a combination that made him a highly sought after spokesperson in media and print advertising. They even had dimples on the right cheek. The same almond-shaped eyes. The same pert nose. Only the slight fullness of their lips, the curliness of their hair, and eyes the color of emeralds hinted that Reign gave them half of their DNA.

"They are absolutely beautiful." Devesh said, tweaking Leena's nose and ruffling Kamran's hair. The twins' hearty giggles caused Devesh to laugh in kind.

His family and the other patrons of Tiffin suddenly became more interested in this unlikely reunion than in the fine cuisine the place offered.

"So, you're married?" he asked, picking the children up as he stood, with absolute no protest from the twins. If the gleam in their eyes told anything—they were elated to be near him.

"No," Reign whispered. She closed the distance between them, intent on extracting her babies from his hold. "I've never been married."

"I didn't realize you were dating back when we ..."

Reign witnessed a range of expressions flitter across his face, signaling that he was trying to sync up timelines and possibilities. He glanced at the children in his arms, inspecting their features before he frowned. No doubt he was recalling the night the two of them had shared a little over five years ago. Her mind followed suit.

A week before the Advertising Age Convention, Devesh had injured his leg during an accident caused by another member during a workout at a fitness center. He was ordered to stay off his feet for at least two weeks. Devesh had a commitment to the companies that sponsored his appearance. Backing out at the last minute wasn't something he would do. Friends and acquaintances, including Reign, banded together to assist him during that week. She arrived at the convention with the Intellectual Property attorneys from the law firm where she worked, but managed to inform the woman putting Devesh's schedule together that she could help at night. All of the friends took turns, whenever time permitted, to make sure Devesh let his body heal from the day's efforts and strengthen enough so he could carry out his duties for the next day.

Reign pulled the "night shift" and brought him some meds, several ice packs for his leg, then massaged those aches when needed. Devesh had asked her to stay a while so they could talk about the things that transpired over the two years after Vegas when they hadn't been in contact. Getting reacquainted led to a host of conversations that lasted well into the night. Time slipped away from them, and when the clock struck midnight, Devesh said, "Why don't you stay here with me." He gestured to the opposite side of his bed.

"Oh, that's pretty slick trying to get me in the sack," she replied with a laugh. "Are we doing that one leg on top of the covers thing?"

"Woman, I don't have to play games when it comes to my feelings for you," Devesh countered and his tone was dead serious. "I want you in the best and worst way. But I have control and so do you. It's late. Having someone see you tip out of here might cause a few tongues to make something out of nothing. The lawyers you work for are here."

She hesitated a long moment. Truthfully, it wasn't him she was worried about. She had fallen for him before because he had shown her more love, compassion, and consideration than any man before. Finally, he ended her confusion and misgivings by saying, "Go on, Reign. I'll call you if I need anything. I promise." She knew he wouldn't. The others had already let her know he was stubborn, overexerting himself and not taking the injury seriously. She opted to stay.

On night two, when he asked her to stay again, she woke when he touched her, beckoning for her to move toward him. He slept with his arms around her, spooning her in an intimate embrace that made her feel safer and more loved than she had ever been. She also watched him as he slept, noticing he was resting better than he had the night before.

Night three and four were more of the same. Night five was a mind-blowing, next-level sensual experience neither one of them could have foreseen, but Reign welcomed it with everything she had to give. Yet, the next morning Devesh's expression was solid and purposeful as not a word passed between them about that love-making or how close they'd become. Actually, he seemed to forget everything that had happened. She laid her head on the pillow and closed her eyes for a moment. When she opened her eyes again, he was gone. The rejection was so profound, she vowed no one would ever have that power over her again.

"You have to come back to the house," Devesh said, snapping her back to the present. "We need to talk."

The children had a vice grip on his neck. Two identical pairs of green eyes pleaded with her to say yes, then Leena, the more talkative of the twins took things a step further. "Please, Mommy. Please ..." while Kamran nodded his support of that request.

"I'll see if I can make time to come," she whispered.

The twins' joy spilled over in the form of chuckles that brought smiles to the lips of the few family members who circled Devesh, fascinated by the children. Especially delighted was Devesh's twin Anaya, whose beauty matched his handsomeness measure for measure. Reign remembered the family member's faces as Devesh consistently posted photos of all Indian holiday celebrations, birthdays, and family gatherings on social media. She also remembered that each of them had been extremely vocal in their opposition to Devesh's desire to pursue a relationship with her.

"How is Jay?" Devesh asked, referring to her older son.

"He just graduated from Columbia," she replied, trying to keep her voice steady. "He's building his portfolio."

Devesh and Jay had become close during those first two years of Reign's and Devesh's friendship. Though her son was loyal to her, she told Jay that she didn't see a reason for his relationship with Devesh to end simply because she wasn't having anything to do with him. Her son was careful to keep any information about Devesh to himself, although there were many times when she wanted to ask. The twins were a huge secret for Jay to keep, which said more about her son's need to keep the relationship with Reign intact, than to jeopardize it by breaking his promise to her.

Now she would be unable to take the coward's way out. And if the pointed looks Devesh's family shot their way were any indication, the members of the Maharaj family were going to give voice to the main question long before Devesh could demand answers he was fast becoming aware he should ask.

The twins had inherited Reign's uncanny sense of observation early on. They now eyed her with keen interest, as though they sensed that her present anxiety was related to Devesh.

"Can I put you down for a moment?" he asked the children.

The twins shook their heads and tightened their hold, causing Devesh to put an intense focus on Reign, blinking as though still trying to get an understanding. His lips parted to speak and Reign braced herself. Then Devesh grimaced, clamped his mouth shut and shook his head.

Devesh's mother, Jasinder, had an eagle-eyed gaze locked on Reign. She lifted her left eyebrow, posing a question of sorts or giving Reign the opportunity to confess.

She knows. My God, she knows.

Reign transferred her focus to Anaya, who peered at the children, apparently summing up things on her own.

Devesh's father, Suresh, leaned in to his wife, eyebrows drawn in, his face registering his concern at the intensity of the unspoken exchanges taking place around them.

Jasinder formed the sounds slowly enough for Reign to make out five distinct words, "They belong to our son."

Suresh blanched, eyes flashing with fire before a scowl descended on his wide mouth. Then he shook his head as though to rid himself of what those words meant. Both Jasinder and Suresh focused on the children again, who were now holding an animated conversation with Devesh about their day at the amusement park. The accusation behind the curious glances from Jasinder, Suresh, and Anaya galloped Reign's way.

"I'll text you my address," Devesh said to Reign.

Her children. No—*his* children gave Reign a look so intense her knees almost gave out.

Kamran tilted his head as he studied her, probably taking in the tense lines of her face. Leena's lips pursed into a thin line, but it was her eyes that said everything. They knew Reign had no intention of showing up, even at Devesh's insistence.

Devesh leaned down with Kamran in his arm and said, "Hand that to me, little guy."

Kamran quickly plucked the cell from Reign's hand before she could protest. He passed it to Devesh, who manuevered to use the pad of his thumb to scroll down the contact list. "My number's not in your phone?"

Reign parted her lips to defend herself, but shut it because he wasn't done.

"And you blocked me on Facebook too? I don't understand any of that. We definitely need to talk." He looked down at the children, who were so comfortable they still wouldn't let him go. "I thought we were friends, Reign," he whispered so his family wouldn't hear. "That we were close. How could you disappear on me like that? How could you …"

The unspoken words *"not tell me that you had my children"* hung in the air.

Reign reached for Leena, and her daughter shrank back, and laid her head on Devesh's chest instead.

An unexpected pain seared Reign's heart. "I had my reasons."

"You should ride with them, Devesh," a voice behind them encouraged. "Make sure they arrive safely."

Reign turned, upset that Jasinder would try to box her in by voicing such a suggestion. A petite woman with a salt-and-pepper braid flowing down her back, came forward to stand next to Jasinder. The woman gave Reign a calming smile and a slight bow of her head as if Reign was royalty; the only one standing with Devesh's family who wasn't glaring at Reign as though she had committed a crime.

"Would you like for me to ride with you?" Devesh asked the children. They approved vehemently.

"Looks like they agree," he said with a victorious lift of his chin as he studied Reign's face.

"Papa."

Oh, sweet Jesus. No. No. No.

Devesh's attention snapped to Leena with that one word before he peered at Reign. "Wow, I must look a lot like their father for her to say that."

"Imagine that," his mother said, and her tone was every bit sarcastic as Devesh's had been. "He definitely must be East Indian, yes?"

Reign paused, tamping down a weary sigh. "Yes, he is."

"They look like they might have some Maharaj blood somewhere along the line," she mused, stroking a weathered finger across Leena's cheek.

Reign saw the seed taking root deeper in Devesh's mind. He was silent as he put his focus on the children.

"Reign," Devesh said, taking her attention from his mother's hard glare. "Come. Let's go."

"I won't be able to stay long."

Devesh exchanged a speaking glance with his mother, possibly alarmed by the change in her demeanor. Jasinder's stony expression was a sure sign of displeasure. Whether it was in response to Reign's statement or because she was well aware that some major deception was going on remained to be seen.

The smile didn't reach Jasinder's eyes as she said in thickly accented English, "I am certain that a short while is all it will take."

Reign recognized those words for the threat they were designed to be.

CHAPTER TWO

An hour later, the family settled Devesh down on one of the many sofas scattered about in several adjoining rooms. His parents and aunt pulled out the baby photos of him and his twin. Then other family members gave Reign a tour of the nearly eleven thousand square foot oceanfront mansion.

After nearly every family album had been placed before Devesh and Reign in an attempt to get her to acknowledge the obvious, he finally looked over to Reign, gestured to the albums and said, "I am their father."

Reign closed her eyes, trying to calm the fear that had been tap-dancing in her gut since the near silent drive to the place, then walking into a home—actually, mansion—that took her breath away. Evidently, the Maharaj family was wealthy, though Devesh had been so humble that she would never have guessed that was the case.

"Leena is a mirror image of my sister, and Kamran is a reflection of me," Devesh explained with a pointed glare at Reign. "That can't be a coincidence. And they are how old?"

She parted her lips to give a non-answer but nearly choked on the ball of pain lodged squarely in her throat.

"We're four years, six months, two weeks ..." Leena offered

cheerily as she glanced at Kamran who looked up from his Disney watch and finished with, "five days and ...." Leena frowned at Kamran, nudging him as she whispered, "You're supposed to say the hours and minutes, too."

"It keeps changing," Kamran said, scowling at his twin. "I have the hard part."

Reign's lips tightened when Devesh leaned back in his place on the sofa and continued to study her, eyes widened by the undeniable truth. She'd always encouraged the twins to keep up this way because it made them more aware of the importance of numbers. Now they'd given him the exact coordinates needed to map out the answer on his own, without her confession.

"What made you check out on me back then," he whispered, frowning as though trying to make sense of the whys of it all. "And why would you keep my children from me? Did I hurt you in some way?"

"No." She shook her head, alarmed that he would jump to that conclusion. "No, you didn't."

"I thought our night together was so beautiful," he said in a voice that only she could hear. He moved closer to where she stood—a spot that was not too far from the front door. "When I woke that next morning there wasn't one ache or pain in my body anywhere. Everything was right in my world." He cupped her face in his hands. "I was determined to go home and let my family know that I would have you in my life no matter how they felt. And then you weren't there anymore. You didn't say a word. Left me thinking that I was wrong about us—that you didn't love me."

Every word was a stab of pain in her heart.

THE TEARS STREAMING down Reign's face almost touched him. Almost. She had kept his children from him all this time and never once considered how much they— or she—would mean to him.

He sucked in a deep breath to calm his anger. Instead, he felt his body go rigid with remembered pleasure of being with her, and quickly decided it would be best to keep a little distance between them for the time being.

Devesh cast his glance over to the twins. Leena was now in Anaya's arms, and Kamran was on Mumma's lap. The years when he could not reach Reign had been hard on him. And none of it seemed to faze her—not his pain, not the fact that he was hurt even more by her insistence on keeping this secret. This beautiful, but heart-wrenching secret.

"I demand to have equal time with my children," he said when no answers were forthcoming from Reign. His eyes held tightly to hers. "You have had them all to yourself for four, nearly five, years. And I have had none. I demand some time to get to know them. For my family to get to as well."

Reign placed her focus on the twins, who were taking a pointed interested in the private conversation being held between their parents on the opposite side of the room.

"You have done them and me a great injustice, Reign," he said, his voice holding a gravity that mirrored how he felt. "And I demand that you make it right. Give me some time with them—alone." He placed his hands on her upper arms. "Four years would work. Four years, six months, two weeks and five days to be exact, but I'll settle for a couple of hours until we can work things out."

She vehemently argued her point against leaving the children with people they didn't know. This went on for nearly half an hour, and he countered each and every one of her objections before she finally gave up, stared up at him, then snatched from his hold.

"Two hours. Is that too much to ask?"

Reign went to her children, gathered them from his mother's and sister's arms. She held them to her for several moments, then whispered something to each of them. They embraced her and nodded their acceptance of what she had said, but did not look happy.

She gave Mumma an intense look, and when the salt-and-pepper haired woman slowly nodded to the unspoken request, only then did Reign release a resigned breath. She left the house without giving him or anyone else so much as a goodbye. And as much as he wanted to run after her, the anger holding him hostage would not let him. He continued to watch through the foyer's windows as the rental car she slid into drove off and disappeared.

Children. He actually had children. For so long, he thought maybe he was sterile because none of the few women he'd been with had ended up pregnant. Not that he'd been trying to sire a child, but he hadn't exactly been careful about doing what it took to prevent a pregnancy either. But that one majestic night with Reign had been the most powerful and explosive love-making he'd ever experienced. Somehow, it resulted in giving him the one thing that had alluded him for far too long. And it happened with the woman he had fallen for from the first time they'd held a conversation in Vegas.

Though he had witnessed the love that his parents had for each other, marriage had not been something Devesh had wanted early on —until he met Reign. Given his family's rejection of her, before she had even graced their presence, he thought that the union would never be possible. By the time he was prepared to defy them, his ambition had taken a front seat. Travel to other countries and charity work for the orphanages in India helped keep him from obsessing over his family's rejection of Reign. But when he thought about a family, he wanted it with a woman who had it together, who knew how to establish goals and reach them. A woman who was done playing games. He wanted a woman that he could learn from, that he could love, and who would love him not for the way he looked or for his body. Someone who would complement the parts of him that needed it most.

Devesh knew from day one that Reign was that woman, but his family was not hearing him. Especially when Tiya had taken it upon herself to extract a few images of Reign from a social media page. When his mother and father took a look, saw that she wasn't his age and that she wasn't East Indian, they were adamant about Devesh cutting off all ties with her. The argument went on for months before he'd allowed his friendship with Reign to diminish, and he had hated to give in to their wishes. Nothing filled the void that the loss of her had created—not work, not travel, not family. Nothing.

Then they reconnected almost two years later in Atlanta. It felt as if no time had separated them between Vegas and Atlanta whatsoever. This time, he was ready to take on every one of his family's objections

—and he had, vehemently, and won. He called to share the news with Reign, fully prepared to forge ahead with a relationship if she would have him. Silence on her end. Now he wondered if he should have expressed his feelings to her *before* they left Atlanta. Maybe then she would have accepted his calls. Maybe then she would have responded to his emails. Maybe then she wouldn't have disappeared as if he hadn't mattered to her as much as she had to him.

On his birthday, fate had brought them together in a way that neither Reign nor his family had any choice but to accept. And his brutal words had sent her running from his parents' home, hurting in a way he never intended.

Leena looked up at him, a single damning tear streaming down her face, soon followed by several more. She did not look away, and the searing pain in her eyes was not hard to miss.

She had a weary expression that no child should ever wear. Devesh could practically hear her thoughts.

Losing my mother is the price of having a father?

Yes, he had every right to be angry with Reign, but to separate his children from the only parent they had known was downright cruel. Even for a small amount of time.

Leena tugged on her brother's arm, and Kamran followed her to the northeast corner of the house—the wealth corner—where an altar, a Puja, a brightly lit lamp, the scent of sweet incense, and other sacred pieces and scriptures held space.

The two of them settled on the white marble floor, sitting Indian style—lotus position—as though preparing for a private meditation all their own. Kamran placed his arm about Leena's little shoulders in a protective gesture. Devesh had done that same thing with his own twin when they were growing up—two East Indian children transported from a place filled with culture, music, literature and familiar faces and dropped into the busy and fast-paced urban landscape of the Bronx.

His children had their backs to the adults, who all looked on, amazed at their silent solidarity. Leena and Kamran somehow recognized the Puja room, a place where Devesh gave reverence to the Creator every day, as the safest place in the Maharaj home. The twins were very much aware of the purpose of this space, and that touched him. In his culture, God the Creator is considered the true owner of the home, and the people within are simply the caretakers. Puja is a daily reminder that God is supposed to have the most important place in everyone's life, heart, and mind. Evidently, Reign had at least exposed them to some aspects of his culture.

The air was tense, filled with the silent condemnation the twins were too young to speak. He had done them a disservice, and now his children were making their displeasure known. Devesh could only wonder what kind of prayers his children were sending up at the moment. Especially since he, a man who he wanted them to love and trust, had already hurt them. The fact that the twins felt the need for God's assistance caused a sliver of anguish to run through him. He would make this right.

Devesh crossed the distance from the family room and into the living room, lowered to his knees and settled in the space behind his children at the Puja, who did not bother to turn around and acknowledge his presence.

"I will go and find your mother," he whispered.

Only then did Leena look over her shoulder, slowly, as though considering those words and the person who said them. She gave a single nod then put her focus back to the Puja. Kamran, obviously the more stubborn of the two, did not acknowledge him at all. The firm set of his shoulders was saying everything that needed to be said. He did not appreciate the way his father had treated his mother, and he would not be swayed as quickly as his sister.

"I promise to bring her back," Devesh vowed. "Kamran, will you look after your sister for me?"

Seconds passed before Kamran's body angled to face him, but only slightly. He peered upward into Devesh's eyes as he said, "I take care of Leena." He nodded then as though that was the end of the subject.

So serious for someone so young. What had they been through? What did he really know about Reign?

"Thank you."

Kamran took his sister's hand before putting his focus on the altar again.

Devesh stood, thoughts whirling of what he would say to Reign when he laid eyes on her again. Without another thought, he snatched up his keys and marched to the door. His youngest sister's voice rang out loud and clear. "So already we have to take care of your little half-breed bastards?"

He froze with one foot halfway over the threshold. Anger rippled through him so quickly he couldn't send a message to his brain that he should keep marching toward his mission and ignore that taunt. He was in Tiya's face within ten strides that ate up the carpet.

"Don't you *ever* insult them that way," he snarled, while Anaya tried to put a solid grip on his arms and hold him back.

"Well, that's what they are," Tiya countered, putting a few inches of space between them. She almost tripped over the long, flowing strands of dark hair that touched past her ankles.

Aunt Kavya turned an icy glare to Tiya, then looked to Devesh before placing a calming hand on his arm.

"Yes, they are of mixed parentage," he agreed. "But you meant it as an insult beyond that, and I'm taking it as one. Keep a civil tongue when you have anything to say about my children."

She blew him off with a shrug. He realized that if Tiya could give voice to this kind of anger, then leaving his children there would not be a good thing.

"Leena. Kamran. With me," Devesh said, extending his hand toward them.

The children were by his side in the time it took to blink. Each flanked him and took hold of one of his hands. Both of them glared at Tiya as though they understood that she had said something improper about them and it was the reason Devesh was not pleased.

"Son, go," his mother encouraged, leaving her position next to his father and moving into a place in front of Devesh. "I will look to their well-being. Go to her." She placed a hand on his cheek. "They need her. And *you* need her. They should not hear the conversation you will have with their mother."

"Mumma ..." he began, using an East Indian endearing word for mother, before sweeping a look across the silent members of his family who donned expressions that ranged from indifference to curiosity to slightly hostile. Except Aunt Kavya, who smiled.

As though sensing the reason for his concern, Mumma added, "I will take care of them myself. I promise you."

Devesh lowered until he was eye level with his children. "I'm going to your mother, and I'd like for you to stay with my Mumma. Alright?"

The twins took a searching glance at Mumma, whose smile wavered a bit as she tried to be reassuring. Then they scanned the faces of everyone else in the room who stared back at them. The twins tightened their grips on his hands, then released them as they moved forward and reclaimed their positions in front of the Puja.

Evidently, they had a survival instinct that was more intact than his own. And they trusted each other more than they trusted anyone else. Hopefully, that would change over time.

With one last warning look at his youngest sister and a reassuring nod from Mumma, Aunt Kavya, and Anaya, Devesh was out the door and on his way to an uncertain future.

CHAPTER THREE

Reign's heart was so broken she didn't know if it could ever be mended. He hated her for what she'd done. She was certain of that one thing. And he had every right to feel that way.

She had taken the easy way out, all because she feared that Devesh would reject the children as he had rejected her—just like Jay's father had done.

Reign never realized Devesh came from a wealthy family. All this time she believed him to be a struggling aspiring actor who welcomed her help to get his career moving in the right direction. The minute she set foot in the Maharaj home, any myth she'd bought into about him had disappeared so fast it was as if it had never been there.

Though Devesh was loaded, he had the humility and compassion of a man who had grown up on the poorer side of life and didn't hold the world responsible for any shortcomings.

She thought she'd been so clever by setting up an estate plan that contained explicit details for the children's care into the age of majority and a letter explaining their existence to a father who would be blindsided by the news. The letter also explained why she felt it necessary to withhold the information that he was the father of two precious children. No need for such a letter or to keep putting money in those trust funds now.

The Maharaj home exuded an unforgettable ambiance from the moment she crossed the threshold. The display of wealth was extremely unsettling, as it brought the reality they had enough money to give her a serious custody battle. That thought was the only reason she had given in to leaving the twins with him for those two hours. Denying him would have made the situation worse.

She dropped down on the bed and rummaged through the tote bag until her cell was in her hand.

First, she tried to reach her friend Renee, but she was in the middle of counseling a client. Then she tried for Debra who said, "Let me call you back later, love. The massage therapist is here." Deb's efforts at regaining full range of motion after a hip replacement was definitely more important than Reign's unburdening of her soul.

Reign then dialed Janice, who informed her that she was in the lawyer's office finalizing the details of gaining her freedom from a man who had not seen her value for nearly two decades.

She held the phone for several minutes before making a call to the one person who knew almost as much about her situation with Devesh as she did.

"Jay, I messed up so bad," she admitted.

"Mama?" he said, and she could tell she had woken him from a daytime nap. He worked on design projects mostly at night, as there weren't so many distractions. "Mama, what's wrong?"

"I ran into Devesh today," she said, her voice barely a whisper. "He … he's going to take them from me."

"Mama, calm down," he admonished, and she heard a rustle of what had to be bed linens in the background. "He wouldn't do that."

"You didn't see him. You didn't *hear* him," she cried, gripping the edge of the bed. "He's so angry with me, it's not even funny."

"Where are the munchkins right now?"

"With his family. He asked—no, he demanded—that they spend time with them today." She mentally flipped through the images of the Maharaj mansion including the billiards room, pub-style bar, temperature-controlled wine room; and her worries intensified. "The man is rich, Jay. He has the kind of money that could tie me up in court for years. I don't have the kind of funds it'll take to fight him."

The majority of her money had been dropped into their college and trust funds. Basically, for the first time in a long time, she was living paycheck to paycheck in a job that was merely helping her make ends meet before she met the end. And though his house and family would benefit her children on a number of levels, and it seemed Devesh could give the twins things she couldn't afford, splitting their time between California and Chicago was not going to be the best thing for them.

"Mama, I think you're buying a problem before it's even been sold," Jay said in a voice that irritated her because it was so calm and rational. He was always the voice of reason, and she could swear she didn't know where he came by that trait. Jay was so unlike her in many ways. And definitely unlike the father who had abandoned him early on in life. All the hurt and pain her oldest son had endured from his absentee father was heartbreaking enough. Reign was determined that the twins would not be subjected to that kind of hatred.

"You're not going to say I told you so."

Jay was silent for a moment before he answered, "I don't need to. You did what you thought was best, but now you'll have to get used to doing something different. You'll need to share them with him. You'll just have to find out how it can be done in a way you can live with. They are his children too, Mama," he said in a low tone. "I never understood your stance on this because you definitely weren't like this when it came to me. You told my father straight out of the gate. Anytime I wanted to see him, you would drop whatever you were doing and take me to his mother's place where he's been living since Hector was a pup—and Hector's a big dog right about now and Dad is *still* living with his mama. If I was on punishment, you took me off long enough to spend time with him." Again he didn't say anything for a second, and then, "I appreciate the fact that you never kept me from him. You never said a negative word about him. I found out what a deadbeat he was on my own."

Reign had tried her best not to put his father's trifling ways on blast and to make sure that Jay had some positive male presence in his life. She'd put him in martial arts because it had a multitude of strong men as mentors, and she'd even landed a big brother for him through the Big Brothers Big Sisters of Metropolitan Chicago. She had grown up with a father who went out for a Pepsi and some smokes and he didn't return until twelve years later—with another set of children and a mistress in tow. The family had been devastated by his absence when it first happened. With the breadwinner missing in action, the family went so far down, they didn't know there had ever been an up. Their mother, Thelma, a housewife who didn't have a high school diploma or skills that could hold a job that would support six children, never knew what would happen from one day to the next.

The Latino family next door, were in the same state as Reign's family. The father had left the seven of them. They were poor but not quite on the level of Reign's family. So the two mothers began to share resources and survived that way. That is, until Roberto, the oldest son of the Madera family, fell for fourteen-year-old Reign, and she became pregnant.

Thelma put a suitcase filled with only a few of Reign's things outside the front door and said she couldn't come back unless she agreed to have an abortion. When Reign picked up that suitcase and made it halfway up the concrete pathway to the sidewalk, Thelma quickly amended her stance. "Since you're so hell-bent on keeping the baby, you can return under *one* condition."

Maria was forced to intervene and give Reign a place to stay right after that "condition" placed by her mother went in a direction Thelma never intended. She had to stand in front of the members of the congregation—and apologize for her sin. The process didn't go well for Reign's mother or the pastor.

Thelma, still upset about being ostracized from the church she had been a member of for most of her life, unleashed her rage on Maria for helping Reign. She called her a *spic*. Maria saw Thelma for what she really was—a hypocrite—and told her straight to her face. She hadn't been a *spic* when she put groceries on the table of a house whose cupboards were bare. She wasn't a *spic* when she shelled out money to keep the lights and gas on for Reign's family. Maria wasn't a *spic* when it suited Thelma's needs, but after Maria saw fit to have compassion on a fourteen-year-old who was pregnant by her twenty-one-year old son, she was every name but a child of God.

Roberto turned out to be more like his father than anyone realized. He had been a grown man, seven years older than Reign, yet he blamed *her* for getting pregnant. Not only did he float in and out, making "guest appearances" in Jay's life, but he would also get upset when he finally offered the crumbs of his life and Jay showed him that he wasn't all that hungry. Roberto also had forced Reign into an ugly child support battle that waged all the way up until Jay started college. Over the years, he avoided paying child support—switching jobs, taking menial positions, collecting unemployment, becoming a "professional" student, and attempting to terminate his parental rights, to name a few.

Finally, after an experience where Roberto ducked into the bathroom right before a court appearance to avoid having to see his son, Jay told Reign, "Enough! I'll make it on my own. Stop going to court for this. I'm going to be married with my own children, and you'll still be up in this place trying to get what you feel he owes you. Enough, Mama. Let it go. Let *him* go. I'm certainly going to."

And he was right. The minute she simply left the situation with Roberto having to pay the twenty grand in arrears and nothing more for college, the doors opened for her son to attend Fisk University in Nashville on a presidential scholarship, then South Carolina State before finishing up years later with a graphic design degree from Columbia College in Chicago.

"I know that my father not being in my life was his choice, not yours," Jay explained. "You didn't give Devesh a chance to do right by his children. You made it *your* choice, not his," he warned, and the truth was a little hard to bear. "Somehow, it seems like the Universe wants you to do something about that."

Yes, her oldest child was right about that, too.

CHAPTER FOUR

Anaya Singh Bakshi watched her twin rush from the living room. Her focus went to the two children who were suddenly thrust into a world that had more questions than answers. They were positioned in the same place their father chose for meditation and answers each day. Anaya had a feeling that the entire family needed to go to the Puja and join the two little ones in whatever quest they were on at the moment.

This situation, though, had the entire family shaken. No one in the Maharaj family had married outside of their culture. And for Devesh to want someone like Reign—a woman who wasn't as young as he was, and who was Black—her parents were holding it together pretty well.

"Well that was intense," her older brother, Bhavin, said. His petite wife, Sana, nodded from her position on the family room sofa.

Conversation among the family resumed, most of it speculation about Devesh's relationship with Reign or lack thereof. The rest was centered around what they believed would come from this new development.

A lot of things had happened in the Maharaj family over the years, but Devesh's desire for Reign, and now the discovery that they have children together, had to be the most scandalous. Things would be

90

different if the more immediate family had been left alone to wrap their minds around the situation before the extended part of the family became involved.

Unfortunately, the Shoreview Mansion was the center of all social activities for the Maharaj family. All of the family, extended family, some of their friends and co-workers paid into a pot that purchased the groceries for dinners that were prepared for everyone on a nightly basis. Mumma, Aunts Kavya, Prisha, and Neerav kept everyone's babies, toddlers, and preschool aged children during the day so that the women in the family could pursue their careers. The nightly dinners also served as a safe haven to discuss many things or for everyone to pitch in to watch the children if a couple wanted to go out on a date or vacations.

When Devesh landed a major role in a Bollywood film, he had used every dime of that money to purchase this home in the warmer climate of California. Then he expanded it according to Mumma and Papa's wishes. That was before moving the immediate family from New York to California—his parents, Anaya and her husband Pranav, his brother Bhavin and wife Sana, sister Tiya and her husband Hiran, uncles Samar and Mitul and their wives Prisha and Kavya, along with cousins Neerav and Meenu. Soon, a few others followed and settled in homes in nearby suburbs. All of them were in the house at the moment, as they had come to celebrate Devesh and Anaya's birthday. The day started at Disney Land, Devesh called it the "happiest place in the world." The party at the house would normally continue well into the next morning, but no one was in a festive mood at the moment.

"I have never seen Devesh so angry," Papa said, concern etched in his tawny face.

Papa was wrong. Devesh had been livid several years ago after the ugly things some of the family members said about Reign when he told them he had every intention of marrying her. Tiya had taken the liberty of stalking Reign's social media pages and printing pictures for all of the family to see. She deliberately pulled ones that were not the professional images that Anaya had seen, when she too, had sought to find out more about the woman who had captured her brother's heart. No other woman had made Devesh want to take that trip into holy matrimony. Not even the blonde "starlet" he'd had an on again-off again relationship over the years.

Anaya extracted herself from the flurry of people holding multiple conversations, wound her way into the kitchen to pour two small glasses of fresh mango juice. She placed them on a tray then journeyed through the series of open rooms the family called the four corners—a den that led into a family room which led into the living room and parlor—before sliding it toward Devesh's children.

"No, thank you," Kamran said, looking up at her with green eyes so expressive that Anaya wanted to take him in her arms and make up for all the hugs she hadn't been able to give him.

"You must have something, little one," Anaya whispered, stroking a hand through his hair.

"No thank you, ma'am," Leena said, her eyes glazed with tears. "We'll wait for Mama and Papa."

"She said drink," Uncle Mitul roared all the way from the den, causing the children to flinch. His face was a mask of unconcealed fury. He had always been loud and brash, but never to the many Maharaj children when they were sitting on his lap as he told them stories or gave them treats and gifts.

"They are children," Tiya snapped, her fist shaking in the air.

"Why are we deferring to what they want?" Uncle Mitul asked. "They should do as we say."

"No thank you," Kamran said more forcefully, moving to be in front of his sister as though to protect her with his little body. "We will wait."

Silence descended over the room again. These children had commanded the attention of everyone. They were beautiful and had a strength about them that belied their tender ages.

"Leave them be," Papa said in a tone that caused everyone to turn toward him. "They are my grandchildren. If they do not want to be bothered—Leave. Them. Be."

Leena used Kamran's shoulder to pull herself up from her spot in front of the Puja. She made a beeline through the parlor and living room, then went straight for Papa and wrapped her arms around his legs. Kamran was right on her heels, but he went to Mumma instead.

Papa's dark brown eyes widened with shock, then he melted with an expression; something so pure that it touched Anaya's heart. Papa's hand reached out to stroke the silky hair that was so like Anaya's had been as a child. The little girl looked up at him with eyes filled with gratitude and love.

The fact that the twins were well aware of which people in the house were in their corner spoke volumes. Papa, normally the more talkative of Anaya's parents, had not said much. Until now.

Everyone had been elated when the passion Devesh felt for that woman died down. Now she was back, and if the anger rippling through her brother was any clear sign, he was still in love with her. Angry, but the love was still there.

When Devesh made the transition to product spokesperson, Reign had helped him in minor ways that brought him a small amount of success. Anaya hadn't envisioned that Reign could be in her brother's life in any capacity, except as a friend. But as Devesh talked about her more and more, in ways he never had with any other woman, his tone was so enthused and inspired, that for a minute, Anaya became alarmed.

Then she took a peek on Reign's Facebook page and quickly dismissed her as a threat to any plans their family had for him. Reign was an exotic beauty in her own way, but plain in comparison to the model types her brother was used to dating. Even the Maharaj women were beautiful enough to participate in pageants, and almost all of them had trophies and landed scholarships that furthered their college education as part of the prizes. Reign was more the motherly, nurturing kind of woman. So yes, friendship was the only thing there could ever be between her and Devesh.

The tide turned when the family voiced their concerns over the fact that Devesh was spending too much time on the phone with her, texting, calling, video chatting—all innocent; mostly business. So they thought. But there was something about the vibe Devesh had after speaking with her that Anaya recognized as something she'd only seen in one other person. Herself, when she fell in love with Pranav.

But Devesh was intensely steeped in their culture. He knew what was expected of him. He could "play" with foreigners all day long, take them for a test drive if need be, but even he understood that he'd better ride home with an Indian woman for that life-long marital journey.

Though he had dated women of other ethnic backgrounds, none of them had been Black. None of them had been older. None of them had been so ... thick. That was the word—the woman was curvy. What were they calling it these days? Plus size. How could he be attracted to her? So the blonde aspiring actress didn't hold his interest anymore? He had to sleep with a grown woman with some years on him? And she managed to get pregnant? How irresponsible!

Anaya swept a look to the twins, who were listening to a story that Papa was sharing to keep them entertained. All the other family members had gone back to eating and gossiping but were sending looks at the children, watching how Papa, Aunt Kavya, and Mumma seemed to be at ease. Even her husband, Pranav, was smitten by them.

She could swear it took everything inside of her not to scream "DNA test." Honestly, there wasn't a need for one. Those children didn't look like they took any genes from Reign other than her green eyes and a little fullness about the lips. They did seem to take her determination, strength, and intelligence, though.

Leena scrambled down from Papa's lap, cornered one of the coffee tables and stopped in front of Anaya. She tilted her head back until she could look her directly in the eyes. A small smile played about her little lips. Whatever Anaya's misgivings, they didn't matter at this point.

Anaya brushed aside all thoughts and reached down to take Leena in her arms.

"I'm your Aunt Anaya."

"Anaya," Leena repeated, placing a hand on her aunt's cheek. "Anaya is pretty. Like my Papa."

"That's because your Papa is my brother."

Leena blinked twice, absorbing that tidbit of information. She flickered a look to her brother and then back to Anaya. "Like Kamran ..."

"Yes," Anaya said, smiling at her niece's perception. "Like Kamran is your twin brother, Devesh is mine."

Leena returned that smile and Anaya's heart swelled with love.

Devesh had said he'd wanted marriage and a family, but it wasn't high on his list of things to accomplish. Now she was looking down at his child, and the family had not been silent since he ran out the door, all voicing their opinions on his choice for a mate.

If she, who loved her brother dearly, couldn't accept Reign, how on earth would they?

Download your copy today

https://books2read.com/Lovingmeforme

REBIRTH: STEPPING

I'm Not Supposed to be Here

"Always remember that striving and struggle come before success in the dictionary." — Sarah Ban Breathnach

There was a girl that looked like a rat but blossomed into a chocolate drop and ultimately a phoenix. Her life wasn't easy by any means, but then most tales, the ones that matter, always start that way.

The story is mine, and the chapters within are like puzzle pieces thrown against the fabric of time in many ways. Some fell near my feet like the pieces of my heart. Others I found along the way, like breadcrumbs feeding a soul forever starving for the attention of a mother that chose addiction over me.

Maybe by the end, you will look upon these pages and my past as a map across the dangerous waters of life. Perhaps you will see as the pieces evolve. In the end, the picture may be different from where you started but just as valuable.

Not all angels have wings. I count myself fortunate to have known not one but quite a few in my lifetime. I was born to a drug-addicted mother, so the odds were already stacked when I took my first breath. Everyone thought I was bound to have congenital disabilities and emotional and developmental delays.

Combine that with a father who spent most of those early years in prison and the armchair psychologists had me all figured out—predestined to repeat my parents' mistakes, unable to learn the simplest of things. To hear them tell it, my breaths and days were numbered. But then, isn't that how a phoenix is made?

But they didn't know the band of angels watching out for me. I read somewhere that many of us are here because of a grandmother's prayers. Gigi, Glama, I could go on about the nicknames and terms of endearment that we all give to the family's matriarch, but their mission remains the same. My Grandma's hands were warm with life and a wealth of love for all two-point-five ounces of me.

My first angel came when I was born. Weighing 2.5 pounds at St. Luke Presbyterian hospital in 1980, the fact that I even survived birth is a miracle. I've listened to my grandmother, and godmother tell the story many times. The storytelling began at family gatherings, as sunlight, cocoa butter, and barbeque perfumed the air.

Aluminum foil pans of potato and Macaroni salad joined the bottomless bowls of chips and pretzels on one end of the table. Cake stands filled with all kinds of desert lined another. The faint smell of freshly cut pineapple wafted in the air, indicative of the prized hand-churned pineapple sherbet that ended every family function. Kids my age and older hovered around that table, sneaking fingerfuls of icing before running off to continue a game of freeze tag or another dance contest, all under the watchful eyes of their mothers. I'd walk up, hug, and say hello to my godmother, and she'd respond with,

"You're a pretty little girl." She'd say while shooting a knowing look to my grandmother.

My grandmother often chimed in with, "Yes, she is."

Then my godmother said, "We weren't always sure how you'd look. When you were first born, you looked like a little rat."

My eyes always lowered when she said that. All I could picture were the little newborn rats I'd seen in my science book, then my grandmother would interject. "Yes, you looked like a little rat when you first came out. You didn't have any hair, no eyelashes, no nothing. Just a little body with a heartbeat and a brain."

"Yeah, like a bald little rat," my godmother said with a chuckle.

"But suddenly…," my grandmother's voice turned sweet. That change in tone was my godmothers' cue to nod and agree.

"It's like God took a pencil and started to draw."

"Um-hum," they'd say together.

"Every day, I went to the hospital to see you, and every day it was something new." My grandmother said, "One day you didn't have eyelashes, then I came back, and you had eyelashes. One day no eyebrows, then the next day, eyebrows. Before I knew it, you had a little brown face."

She'd turn to look at me and smile before my godmother chimed in.

"Yeah, the nurses called you 'Chocolate Drop.'"

Then they hugged me, patted me on the behind, and sent me on my way. Somehow, a micro-preemie born in 1980 survived, but my initial struggles set the stage for many challenges in my life.

Fear for me never came in the guise of a vampire or werewolf or giants as one would find in children's books. Part of me would have welcomed the imaginary one. The real ones made you cry. The human ones made you scream.

Someone broke into our apartment on Lawndale Avenue in Chicago when I was five. With nothing but the clothes on our backs, my mother packed us up and flew us to California. As my mother worked through her issues, we were like nomads moving from one place to another. I found out later her 'grown up' problems began and ended with an addiction.

Another angel swept into my life on the day a drug dealer severely beat my mother. Since I wasn't old enough to be left home alone during the day, Mom took me with her when she went to score drugs. That day, she sent me to the taco truck with three dollars to get some rolled tacos, a cheap, quick meal. I waited in front of the liquor store just as my mother had instructed.

It's always there in the back of a child's mind when a parent is late coming to pick them up. Sometimes it creeps in like a nagging feeling. After it happens three or four times, it settles over you like a soggy cloak.

She forgot where she left me. I must have forgotten to clean up my toys, or maybe I was too loud, and she got so mad that she just left me behind and…and…

Terrifying images built in my head as I craned my neck to see where she had gone. That same wild fear made my heart cramp in my chest as I hurried down the street in the direction she went.

I wasn't a baby anymore. Babies cried. Little girls whined and wiped their noses on their shirt sleeves.

By the time I reached the end of the parking lot, I was in a dead run. She wasn't there. My heart rattled against my ribcage as reality set in. And then, a familiar blue sportscar pulled up next to me. The vehicle belonged to a man my mother had befriended.

"Get inside." he barked through the rolled-down window before shoving the front passenger side door open.

I started walking towards the car then froze. My mothers' words rang in my head.

Don't talk to strangers, and whatever you do, never get into someone's car even if you know them without them knowing our secret password.

"Where's my mom?" I asked, backing away from the car.

"She's in the mobile home up the street. Now come on," he snapped. I looked toward the place he indicated, and there was my mom covering her face with a shirt.

"Yonne, get in the car with Lars," she ordered before staggering to the mobile home a few feet away.

"No, I want to go with you," I called out as I took a few steps in her direction.

"No, get in the car with Lars. Do as I say. He's going to take you home," she said, wincing as a stranger helped her into the back of the vehicle

By then, I was crying. "Where are you going?" I whined, not knowing what was going on or what happened.

Lars guided me into the front seat of his car, and we followed the mobile home as it pulled out onto the main road. Through the back window of the mobile home, I could see my mother rocking back and forth, still holding that bloody shirt up to her face. We followed the mobile home until we hit the expressway. We turned, but the mobile home continued straight.

"She'll be okay, Yonne. Let's get you home to bed." He said, trying hard to keep the smile in his voice, but all I had to do was close my eyes, and my mother, covered in blood, filled my mind.

Lars took me back to the apartment we shared with him. He put me in bed and told me my mother would be all right. When I was scared, I would rock myself to sleep and say a little chant in my head I'm cold, I'm hungry, and I want my mommy, I'm cold, I'm hungry, and I want my mommy.

The words swirled within me, circling the gaping hole in my heat where my mother should have been. The harder I cried, the more the chant morphed and grew louder than my tears and my heartbeat thumping in my ears as the words swelled in my throat.

I want my mommy, and then I want my granny, I want my granny; I want my granny.

Mercifully sleep found me, and a dream unfolded where God scooped me up in his arms, flew me to Chicago, and put me in my grandmother's bed, where it was safe, warm, and familiar. I don't know how it happened, but my angel came and got me. The next thing I remember, I was in my grandmother's bed.

Many years later, in my late 30s, I told that story to my aunt as we piled into my car for a day of running errands. She had the strangest look on her face as tears gathered in her eyes.

"That was me," she said finally before shifting her focus to the safety of the rushing traffic.

"Huh?" I asked as I quickly divided my attention between driving the car and watching her stumble over the memories.

"Yonne, that was me; I was the one that came and got you, she said, wincing at some private thought. We were in the basement doing hair when the phone rang. Your grandmother spilled into the chair with this look on her face. "We got to go get Yonne." She said, "Something happened to Nire, and we got to go get Yonne." My aunt looked at me with tears leaking from the corners of her eyes.

"Baby, Granny, hung up that phone, went upstairs to her room, and came out with some cash. I threw some clothes in a bag and was on my way to the airport on the next flight out to get you."

My eyes welled up with tears. "It was you? You're my angel?" My voice cracked with emotion. "I swear, Tee, I remember nothing that happened from when I was in Lar's car. I don't know how I got back to Chicago or how much time had passed."

When we got to our destination, as soon as we got out of the car, I walked over to my aunt and wrapped my arms around her, hugging her tightly. I whispered in her ear. "Thank you for saving me."

How could I know that other angels would appear to shelter me from the coming storms in the years to come?

Perspective

The actions of one person can change the life of another. Looking back on the people who chose to show up in my life during a time when I needed them, they are some of the most invaluable people in my life. I refer to them as angels because they appeared suddenly and made a way when there seemed to be no other way. Like pebbles dropped in a lake that ripple for miles away, their minor actions changed the tide of everything around them, whether the person realizes it or not.

Tools that helped me:

Faith, through my angels, I've learned how to have faith. The bible describes faith as the substance of things hoped for and the evidence of things not seen. My angels appeared in my life right when it seemed my confidence was running low or had run out. Through their appearances, I've learned how to strengthen my faith muscles. Even when things don't turn out exactly how I'd like them to, I know everything happens for a reason, and when I need help, an angel isn't too far away.

This book is broken into sections. You'll get a tidbit from my life, the perspective I've gained, and the mental tool that helped me get through my issues. I've used these tools one at a time or in combination. Hell, some weeks, I'll use all of them at various points to help me get through

THE NATIVE LADY ... THE NAVAJO MAIDEN

Capture her... Kill her...
  The Navajo maiden raced across the desert floor and the Indigenous

invaders followed. The walls of the tall red canyons glistened in the sunlight. Hoofbeats from the black and brown horses created a cloud of thick, choking dust that made her eyes burn. The sound of them snorting behind her as they gave maximum effort in the chase made her break into a dead run.

They stole into the village wearing their traditional buckskin and war colors. The eagle feathers in their hair twisted in the breeze. The stories all ended the same way. Shadows loomed on the horizon before the screaming began. The invaders, armed with bows and arrows took what they wanted and killed everything else before slinking back to the shadows with their spears coated in blood.

Adrenaline poured into her veins propelling her forward. She had to make the clearing. The hopes of the Tó'aheedlíinii clan, which was on the brink of annihilation, rested on her shoulders and whatever energy she had left. She hazarded a downward glance at her red dress that matched the colors of the painted desert canyon dust which coated the beadwork she had carefully sewn in place.

"Cut her off at the pass!" the leader yelled as two black horses broke off to the left, cornering her into submission. The other brown horses turned to the right to complete the circle by blocking her only escape route.

"We have her now; she is not going anywhere!"

The Tó'aheedlíinii Lady continued up the steep path leading to one of her favorite places to pray. The smug look of satisfaction on their faces as they closed in made it clear ... the only way out was within.

She turned while uttering the words "Hózhó náhásdlíí."

This phrase is typically used at the closing of a Navajo traditional prayer meaning, "There will be beauty all around."

The Holy People heard The Tó'aheedlíinii Lady's prayer and provided a strong burst of wind to carry her on her downward journey. To her surprise, her dress served as a parachute allowing her to glide to the ground.

She landed on solid ground without an injury preserving the Tó'aheedlíinii clan. The Tó'aheedlíinii Lady thanked the Holy People for her life.

As she dusted off her dress, The Tó'aheedlíinii Lady looked up at the invaders who were glaring at her from the edge of the cliff. They threw down their weapons in disgust and turned their horses for home.

The Navajo Tribe is a matrilineal society passing clans through a woman. Since The Tó'aheedlíinii Lady was the last female member of the Tó'aheedlíinii clan, she was able to revitalize the clan making it one of the largest Navajo clans. The Tó'aheedlíinii Lady was the epitome of resiliency, faith, and bravery. Those elements remain with the clan to this very day.

War within various tribes resulted in one thing ... they tried to wipe us from the face of this earth. But we're still here. People who are a true testament to what's done in the dark will find its way to the light. Today, I am, a proud member of the Navajo Tribe bringing the story of the First Nation and my trials, tribulations, and triumphs to the light. What happened to my people then, and decades later when outside invaders set foot on North American soil, is the original "cancel culture" some would like to forget, and others have whitewashed or downplayed in history books.

However, the history books do not give the entire account, especially with people wanting to do away with critical race theory and other methods of holding mainstream society accountable for their actions. If you ever want to know how people—who have experienced atrocities that no human should be subjected to—can bounce back, ask an indigenous person what had been done to them. The ancestors provided indigenous people the strength and wisdom to persevere and push forward no matter what.

My history begins with her leap of faith. My story begins with my own. Within these pages, my raw and unfiltered version of growing up Indigenous on or near the Navajo Reservation will be shared. Some people think indigenous people in the United States do not exist, but we are 1.7 percent of the United States population and in every part of American society. We *are* American History.

As indigenous people, we cannot be canceled because *we are woven into the names of cities, states and areas throughout America.* We are often associated with those who live in teepees with no access to technology and the outside world. People typically assume indigenous people still live in the Old West.

We are represented as either savages or some lone figure sitting on a horse with a single tear creasing our cheek or some mascot for a sports team. Rarely, if ever, are we represented truthfully. When someone meets a person like me—clean-cut, freshly pressed clothes, ex-military, and speaks the King's English, they are shocked. People, like myself, live in a modern homes, have advanced degrees, and have lucrative careers. Indigenous people have made great contributions to making society a better place to live for all cultures, not just our own.

Since our values have not been publicized, it is easy to assume we only exist in a historical context. When examining textbooks, we are given a small section that talks about our history, with an overt focus on the conquest versus the beauty of culture. We have a lot more to offer than films about cowboys and Indians, stereotypical sports mascots, and the "drunken Indian" image.

"Our Navajo language and culture matter. It is a direct link to our culture. When we sing Navajo traditional songs in a ceremony, we are retelling our history from the beginning of time," my Uncle Johnny would say whenever we talked about traditional Navajo ceremonies.

I think back on my childhood and my family and all they endured and all the wisdom they instilled in me. I think of my grandfather sitting in his favorite chair after a long day's work. I think of my Uncle Johnny and my mother, father, and even my sisters trying desperately to navigate our past and a future unfolding before us.

Within each of them was a story so intricately woven to mine, that even in the times when sadness, addiction, and oppression threatened to claim one or more of us, there was always an underlying sense of love, respect, and honor that resonated within them, and ultimately within me.

Uncle Johnny served in the Army during the Vietnam War and returned to become a Navajo Nation Police Officer. Later, Uncle Johnny worked at Peabody Coal Mine as a mechanic and then retired. After his retirement, Uncle Johnny became a medicine man (healer) who is as wise as anyone with a medical degree.

"What we do matters in this world, we have a relationship with nature which puts us on a different level with the Creator," he explained. "Our prayers are strong because our people are strong and can handle a lot."

Becoming a Navajo Medicine man takes years of mentorship and internship. Medicine Men take on great responsibility in understanding the Navajo Traditional ceremonies and songs. In traditional Navajo society, Medicine People are considered "gurus" because they possess a considerable amount of traditional knowledge based on oral tradition committed to long-term memory.

When they perform a ceremony, they essentially recite *everything* from memory which contributes to their overall intellectual ability. Traditionally trained and orientated Navajo people have a deep unique understanding of how the universe originated, which is different from the Big Bang Theory, or biblical understanding. This is not to say those systems of thoughts and beliefs are not important, but a traditional belief provides a different perspective.

"It is very important to live a good life and do what is right to stay in harmony," Uncle Johnny explained.

"What does it mean to live a good life?" I asked him at one point.

"It means, you're honoring our ancestors and the Holy People. It is the Holy People who made life possible for the life to begin."

Navajo people passed through three different worlds and into the present fourth world with the aid of the animals and Holy People which are a group of deities. The Navajo believe there are two classes of beings which are the Earth and the Holy People. It is believed the Holy People taught the Earth People how to live the correct way and conduct themselves. They were taught to live in harmony with Mother Earth, Father Sky, as well as animals, plants, and insects.

The Holy People placed four sacred mountains in four different directions with Mt. Blanca to the east (*Alamosa, Colorado*), Mt. Taylor to the south (*Grants, New Mexico*), San Francisco Peak to the west (*Flagstaff, Arizona*), and Mt. Hesperus to the north (*Durango, Colorado*). The four directions are represented by four colors: White Shell represents the east, Turquoise in the south, Yellow Abalone in the west, and Jet Black in the north.

In general, based on Navajo culture, we emerged from the ancestorial lands of the four corners region of New Mexico, Arizona, Utah, and Colorado. This is very different from the belief that Navajo people crossed the Bering Strait and came from Asia.

Navajo clanship has its understanding of how their clans emerged from different parts of the region on the Navajo reservation. Based on traditional knowledge, the Tó'aheedlíinii clan, which is my maternal and primary clan, translated as "Water Flows Together", emerged from Northern New Mexico at the meeting of two rivers which is located at the bottom of the Navajo Dam reservoir.

It brings peace and joy to understand and embrace this origin. Due to centuries of cultural genocide, other ethnicities may not necessarily know the origin of their people. Overall, we are not from another country, but indigenous to North and South America.

So, you can imagine how well it went when we indigenous people were recently referred to in the media as ... "Something Else."

KING OF DURABIA

"You risked your life for my grandson," Sheikh Aayan said, his voice echoing through the ornate throne room. "Ask for anything and I will see what can be done."

"Well, to be honest, I haven't wanted much," she said with a nervous laugh. "And the only thing I don't have is a husband. But I'd love to have a place here in Durabia, where I can come and go as I please. If that is at all possible."

"Done," the Sheikh said, beckoning to the man who had visited the hospital twice to see about her condition. "Kamran, come."

"Wait. What?" She laughed and rested a hand on her ample bosom. "An apartment, really?"

"Your new husband," he answered with a grand gesture that would have made Vanna White proud. "This is my oldest son."

The man was drop-dead gorgeous. Olive complexion, dark hair, goatee neatly trimmed to perfection, and piercing brown eyes that missed nothing. He was more suited to a fashion runway than a palace. Truthfully, she wasn't sure if it was the tunics, neat beards, head coverings or what. Durabia seemed to have no shortage of handsome men. But the Sheikh's son was a masterpiece, exuding the kind of confidence that came with a man who was certain of his place in the world. His gaze swept across her face with a complexion slightly darker than his olive tone, then quickly covered the distance over her curves, then his lips lifted in a warm, appreciative smile that practically lit up his dark brown eyes and sent heat straight to places that had been dormant since the Queen of Sheba caused King Solomon to lose his entire mind.

Ellena shook her head, clearing her mind of all manner of wickedness that came after that wonderful assessment. "I think you misunderstood. I was joking about the husband part. The apartment, time share or whatever you call them here, that's all I really want."

"You will have both," the Sheikh commanded with a nod of finality no one would dare to question. "A husband and a place here. My son needs a wife and you mentioned you do not have a husband. Problem solved."

"But doesn't he have to give you heirs or something?" She instinctively brought her hands near her belly. "My eggs are old enough to be married and have children of their own by now."

First, a roar of laughter went up from him. A few moments later, it was mirrored by everyone standing around her. Yes, that line was funny, but the one thing she understood was the unfairness of the situation. At least for Kamran. And that was no laughing matter.

The Sheikh waved away that thought. "That will not be a concern. He is unable to give you or any woman children. And a woman of African descent will never sit on the Durabian throne. We are safe on that score."

A shadow of sadness flickered in Kamran's eyes and his skin flushed a shade darker. Ellena tried to read a deeper meaning into his father's words. She still came up with unfair. "So, you just throw him to a random woman because he can't give you an heir? He is still a man. He still has value," she insisted. "A brain, intelligence, and a purpose." She inhaled, trying to tamp down on her anger. "The apartment is fine, Sheikh. Thank you, but I will not be foisted on a man who has no say in the matter. That's downright cruel."

A gasp came from the core of people around them before silence descended in the room. Even Kamran flinched.

The Sheikh's face darkened with anger as he slowly came to his feet. "Are you refusing—"

"Give me nine days—"

All eyes focused on the handsome man, who left his father's side and moseyed toward her like some type of Arabian cowboy. All swagger, no gun necessary.

"Give me nine days," he repeated and moved across the expensive Persian carpet until he stood in front of her, towering over her near six-foot height by three inches of his own. "Nine days for me to show you Durabia, to answer any questions you may have. To let you explore the place, the people, the culture. Then you decide."

Ellena let out a long, slow breath, because staying here permanently, marrying him, would be a lost cause. She loved her job as a personal assistant at Vantage Point. Alejandro Reyes, a "Fixer" of everything from political and corporate espionage, to terrorist attacks, was the absolute best person to work for. And she loved the predictability of her life. Traveling overseas was the most adventurous event in her life. Still, curiosity won out over common sense and she said, "All right. Thank you."

"Now we go about the business of getting to know one another," he said, smiling as though her consent brought him much pleasure. Evidently, he wanted this to happen and the intensity of his gaze bore into her soul. "So that you can make an informed decision, yes?"

She glanced over his shoulder, taking in some of the envious looks a few of the women tried to hide. "Why are you doing this?" she asked him. "Why are you allowing them to serve you up to some foreign woman as if you do not have value?"

"Because I recognize this is God's will," he answered. "And who am I to leave a precious gift unwrapped?"

Her eyebrows drew in, as she tried to decipher the hidden meaning behind his words. The man had a peaceful, confident air but also a playful vibe about him.

"Yes, that was a double entendre." His smile widened and she could swear the heavens opened up and smiled with him.

Good Lord, I'm in trouble.

Chapter 2

"You will stay here tonight," the Sheikh commanded. His firm expression dared anyone to question his decision.

"I am here with my classmates." Ellena tore her gaze from Kamran. "We're supposed to see the sights," she protested. "They're probably worried."

"You will be in good hands with Kamran Ali Khan."

"But —"

"Say thank you, Ellena," Kamran whispered, under the Sheikh's fierce frown.

She shifted her gaze to his, saw the warning in his eyes. "Thank you." Then she gave him the Arabic greeting.

The Sheikh flinched, then refocused as he smiled and replied in kind. He slid back onto the throne. "See, she even knows a little Arabic. The proper way to greet. Now your love of Western culture will be put to good use, my son."

"Can he force me to stay here?" she said in Kamran's ear.

"It would be an insult to refuse his hospitality."

"But I don't know any of the customs here—"

"Shhhhh," Kamran whispered, taking her hand in his. "It is fine. You will be fine."

"He can't just throw you away like this," she murmured, searching his eyes for some form of deception. "You don't know me."

Kamran gave her hand a gentle squeeze and guided her to the foyer under the curious gazes of everyone else. "Ellena, nine days is a long time. Today, I will walk you through the palace grounds and then you will give me your original itinerary. I will be certain to take you every place you had planned to see." His dark-brown gaze lasered in on her. "Will that be all right?"

"That sounds nice, but what about the people I was traveling with? This is a class reunion. I haven't seen some of them in ten years. That's the sole purpose of this trip."

"A few inquired at the hospital," Kamran said, walking past the guards at the pathway leading to the exit. "They know you are with the Royal Family. Come, my mother will have a room prepared for you. Tomorrow, we will check into Jumillah."

"What's that?"

"The most precious hotel in Durabia," he said. "And since it is on a private island, it affords the right kind of seclusion."

She nodded, trying to balance herself. All of this was overwhelming.

"Oh, and we are going to the Durabia Mall for you to pick up a few tunics, all right?"

Ellena stopped walking. "What is wrong with ..."

"You will be interacting with the Royal Family," he said in a patient tone. "You must cover certain ..." He lowered his gaze to the cleavage baring blouse. "*Assets*, accordingly."

She tried to pull away. "It's all too much. It's so fast. What if I make a mistake?"

"You will not. Please do not worry."

Ellena scanned his face again, and could not believe how calm he was, given the circumstances. "Aren't you angry? He just—"

"May I be honest?" he said, and his voice was deep, rich, like the smoothest whiskey.

"Yes. Sure."

"You had me at 'he is still a man. He still has value. A brain, intelligence, and a purpose'."

With that being said, Kamran gave her a slight bow as his mother came forward to guide her into an alcove that led to a suite of rooms. He walked past, leaving Ellena's mind churning in circles.

About *King of Durabia*

No good deed goes unpunished, or that's how Ellena Kiley feels after she rescues a child and the former Crown Prince of Durabia offers to marry her.

Kamran learns of a nefarious plot to undermine his position with the Sheikh and jeopardize his ascent to the throne. He's unsure how Ellena, the fiery American seductress, fits into the plan but she's a secret weapon he's unwilling to relinquish.

Ellena's connection to Kamran challenges her ideals, her freedoms, and her heart. Plus, loving him makes her a potential target for his enemies. When Ellena is kidnapped, Kamran is forced to bring in the Kings.

In the race against time to rescue his woman and defeat his enemies, the kingdom of Durabia will never be the same.

I will die if I stay here …
Shannon's entire family sat at the dinner table enjoying a meal

which took her three hours to prepare, while she mowed the jungle of their front yard, seething the entire time. She stopped to empty the bag but froze when her mother-in-law's voice carried from the open pantry window, "I had to fake a damn heart attack to make this stupid heifer get with the program."

Faked a heart attack? Wait. What?

Monique Hallerin had faked that entire one-month ordeal so Shannan would take over the daunting task of shopping, preparing, cooking, then serving Sunday dinners for fifteen people every week, only to criticize nearly everything that Shannan did. Faked it so Shannan's husband, Zach, would pick up the slack on her bills. All while her brothers-in-law and most of her children parked their lazy behinds at the dining room table every Sunday and didn't lift a finger to help. Shannan was way past tired—exhausted was a better word.

"Guests don't wash dishes," her husband said when she mentioned they could pitch in with clean up. Well, to be honest, neither did he and he hadn't been a guest since they'd said, "I do."

What she should've said on the day they were married, fifteen years ago was, "I don't," then ran past his overbearing mother and four shiftless brothers then out the church doors to freedom.

"I had to fake a damn heart attack to make this stupid heifer get with the program."

Shannan, who had seven children of her own, was now responsible for duties that her mother-in-law had done for most of her non-married life; catering to those grown ass men sitting at her dining room table at this very moment while Shannan was outside doing something she had first asked her husband, then one of them, to do.

Rage hit Shannan full force.

She staggered away from the mower, rushed into the house, ran up the stairs and snatched up her tote. She halted at the threshold of her bedroom for a moment, extracting the small shoebox in the back of the closet. A set of credit cards, passport, birth certificate, social security card, and all the hidden cash found its way into the tote. She glanced at the summer wardrobe spilling over into Zach's side and decided there wasn't anything she wanted to take. She tipped down the rear stairway into the kitchen, snatched the keys from a hook near the door to put as much distance between herself and those people as possible.

Shannan only vaguely heard the youngest of her seven children call her name. Her heart constricted as she ignored them, tears blinding her as she slid behind the wheel of an SUV that was almost a second home. Basketball. Volleyball. Football. Gymnastics. PTA. Never any breaks between or any time for her to simply breathe.

I will die if I stay here.

Those seven words came to mind, summarizing her current status. Something that first hit her when she had the argument with Zach before his family arrived …

"No, my brothers shouldn't have to wash a dish in my house," Zachary had protested without bothering to look up from the current prosthetics project spread out over the basement. "My mother spent a week in the hospital and she can't handle it anymore. This dinner is how we stay close. I don't see what the problem is."

"The problem is, that it's all too much," she replied, putting aside her own work on the latest puzzle she was creating for the daily newspaper to focus more on the conversation that was long overdue. "I'm beginning to dread Sundays. I don't have any day of rest."

"Well, if you gave up that job you've been playing at then you wouldn't be so tired all the time," he quipped.

"I shouldn't have to give up anything," she shot back. He'd always considered the six figures she made from being a Master Cruciverbalist—crossword puzzle creator—frivolous. His career as a prosthetist brought in just under what she did. There had been a bone of contention on that score.

"Then it looks like you're going to be busy." Zachary shrugged. "You'll be alright."

"Wouldn't have to be so busy if you and the boys helped around here," she countered.

"My mother raised five boys on her own and never complained," he said, keeping his focus on the circuitry in his hands.

"And she was on her own because she ran your father off," she replied. "Let's be real about that."

Zachary's face twisted into a mask of annoyance as he glared at her. "I can't talk about this with you."

"I'm done talking. I'm tired," she snapped. "There's going to come a time when I say to hell with it."

Zach paused at the end of the wooden bench, scoffing as he asked, "And where are you going to go? Who's going to be a father to seven children?"

"They have a father," she said, and the sorrow of her reality was heavy indeed. "I need a husband."

The moment Shannan hit the expressway, she wiped her tears with the back of a trembling hand. A startling thought hit her. She could not leave her baby girl in that house.

About *Sugar Ain't So Sweet*

Shannan has no choice but to leave her husband, seven children, and a successful career before someone ends up on the wrong side of the grave. *USA TODAY* Bestselling Author, Naleighna Kai, brings a story of a wife who's been manipulated by her in-laws and husband for the last time and is finally fed up with everything and everyone.

Shannan overhears a conversation that forces her to walk out on her husband, seven children, and a successful career to find a sense of peace that has eluded her for years. She thought fate had been kind in giving her a husband who adored her. But she soon discovered fate had pulled a fast one, as her husband's nearly impossible demands and those from his unrelenting family have pushed her to an edge where there might be no return.

Zach has screwed up—royally. With his family following his lead in not appreciating Shannan, his wife shows him that since he can't respect her presence, she'll introduce him to her absence. Determined to win back the woman who is his anchor, first, he must find a way to deal with his overbearing family and disrespectful children that doesn't cause him to lose more than he gains. **While fighting to win back his wife, he's forced to face some hard truths and family secrets that might mean he'll lose Shannan forever.**

Something about him sent a delicious shiver of anticipation up Joy's spine. That shiver did a little curtsy at the base of her neck, before sliding down and sending a tingle between her thighs. Her lips parted of their own accord as if to speak, but no sound would come. The Welcome Circle, where all the rules were laid out for the total strangers embarking on an unforgettable journey, had already started.

"Rule one … pajamas stay on the whole time," the flaxen-haired host said.

Desperate. The one word centered in Joy's mind followed by a few more. *How desperate did a woman have to be to attend an event simply to experience someone else's non-sexual touch?* She was here, wasn't she? Settled on a sofa in a room filled with people who had come for one purpose—a Cuddle Party, the new wave of safe adult interaction. Everyone played by the same set of rules. The word "no" was met with a comforting phrase, "Thank you for taking care of yourself."

Joy, a single of mother of two, had held onto the article from the *Chicago Red Eye* for nearly a year before deciding to give it a try.

The gentleman had caught Joy's attention as he swept into the room. He removed a large bottle of Southern Comfort from a brown paper bag and set it on the counter as he settled into a spot near the front door. With his back against the wall, he observed the people spread out in several open rooms. The man was stunningly handsome, with piercing brown eyes, and dark silky hair with a small shock of silver right at the widow's peak. His olive skin had been kissed by the sun, and lips that were the most delectable she'd ever laid eyes on. He wore silk, navy-blue pajamas that complimented his tall, muscular physique. She, along with several others, couldn't help but stare.

"Rule two," their host continued. "You don't have to cuddle with anyone at a cuddle party. Ever."

Oddly enough, Joy expected a place filled with outcasts, people who might have been easily overlooked on the dating scene and everywhere else. Not so. Each man was more handsome than the last. The women were either drop-dead gorgeous or girl-next-door beautiful.

The mysterious stranger remained near the door until it was his turn to share his expectations of the event. The panther-like gait commanded everyone's attention as he sauntered to the center of the living room where everyone was assembled.

"My name is Ali Khan," the smooth, baritone sound beckoned Joy from her thoughts. His voice was as sultry as his appearance, and that was saying something.

The moment his intense gaze met hers, any misgivings she'd felt about being there quickly dissipated.

"I'm here because I love the concept, and the rules. There's a freedom here that's sorely lacking in the world."

As more guests finished their introductions, Joy found that a surprising number of women shared one common thread—molestation, childhood abuse, sexual harassment. Their willingness to share something so personal gave Joy the strength she needed to let her guard down—but only a little.

She glanced at Ali again. One of the rules drifted into the forefront of her mind. *If you mean yes, say "Yes." If you mean no, say "No." If you mean "Maybe," say no. You can always change your mind later.*

Without warning, Ali turned his head and stared at Joy. They were connected across the expanse of the room for several seconds before she broke contact and lowered her eyes. Her pulse raced as if she'd run a marathon mile at top speed, and everything within Joy screamed that if asked, she'd give this man an absolute, "Hell yes."

Chapter 2

She is stunning.

Ali was addicted to pleasure. Nothing satisfied him more than giving a woman the ultimate release, and that was second to the kind that happened between her thighs.

One word described the elegant beauty settled—somewhat uncomfortably—on the sofa. Captivating. The women here, including Joy, were hardly the rejects and low-hanging fruit his sons had warned him about. She had a shapely body hidden underneath a long-sleeve, button-down pajama top with matching pants. The color reminded him of mauve sorbet, and it complimented her honey skin. Her raven hair hung in loose curls way past her shoulders. Next, Ali focused on her heart-shaped face with full, perfectly kissable lips and expressive, dark eyes that beckoned to him like a trainer waving a steak in front of a hungry lion.

"My name is Joy," she said. The silky timbre of her voice caused several men in the room to shift slightly. He was no exception. "It's taken me an entire year to show up." She lowered her gaze to the pallet positioned on the floor in the center of the room. "And, I'm glad I'm here."

Joy. The quiet beauty and fluid strength were mere enhancements to her appeal. Her eyes were luminous chocolate orbs that held no secrets. She was like an open book to him. He saw the wariness there, then in a flash it was replaced with a glimpse of certainty, followed by an indicator of acceptance. For him? That thought caused a genuine smile to curl on his lips.

Ali welcomed the idea that the rules left no room for doubt. "Maybe" would be voiced as a "No." No quipping, no explanations, no arguments, no persuasion—a simple "No" and the participant moved on with a simple confirming statement. True power lay in the person that respected the other's boundaries. One look at Joy and he became aware that boundaries and walls were relative. He wasn't sure what led him to come this day, but he was glad he'd followed through.

"I'm not sure what to expect ..." He'd heard her say. Neither did he, but the possibilities had become very intriguing.

Ali remained distant, listening to everyone's story. Some with his eyes closed and his heart open. Last year, this approach had garnered a woman whom he had loved and lost. She'd shared a life story filled with such tragedy that his heart hurt every time he thought about what she'd been through. He'd longed to protect her, but through no fault of his own, he had lost her. Family obligation had caused Reign to break his heart. Not because she wanted to, but because she had no choice. He knew all about familial ties. Thankfully, he was on the flipside of that heartbreak. He wished Reign well and now rejoiced in new possibilities.

Wounded. Betrayed. Strong.

So many vibrations swirled about that woman across the room, but he zeroed in on the two that mattered most. *Survivor. Resilient.*

Those two he could identify with. They echoed in his own life. Ali had never realized he had a "savior complex" until now. Joy had an exotic beauty, and elegance even through the pain that was so clearly etched in her velvet brown eyes. It gave him an overwhelming urge to see her smile.

He thought back to his ready-made life with the built-in wife. Happiness was a constant stranger during that time, thanks to his father. Though he'd understood his father's need to be welcomed back into the family fold, it did little to assuage the bitterness Ali felt at being served up as a physical sacrifice. He'd never wanted the marriage he'd been forced into, nor the burden of carrying his father's penance when he'd married a woman outside of their culture. The sins of the father had indeed been visited on the son.

Ali was a self-made millionaire who had fulfilled all his family's expectations—marriage to a woman from an East Indian family, financial stability, and four children to carry on the Khan name. But that was over. He had no intention of spending the rest of his life in a mediocre marriage he'd never asked for when so many possibilities awaited him. He gained the ire of his father and in-laws when he divorced Sonali, but he had assured them that she would always be financially secure. His duty was done.

Not one for loose ends, in business or his personal life, he had eased Sonali into living a life without him and had no objection when she had run into the arms of the childhood friend.

Now the time had come for Ali to pursue his own happiness, and he had every intention of doing just that.

Dwelling on the past was useless, so he refocused his energy on Joy. No point in trying to hide it. She was the only one he wanted to encounter that night. His mind drifted to thoughts of her lush, sensuous body relaxed in mild supplication, as though the art of seduction seeped from her pores. Her demeanor softened when he introduced himself. That acceptance resonated all over her body as she said the word he'd longed to hear drip from her lips—Yes.

Ali knew then and there—Joy would be his.

Completely.

OPEN DOOR MARRIAGE

THANKSGIVING -
CHICAGO, ILLINOIS NOVEMBER 22—7:23 P.M.

"You slept with my aunt?"

The words still didn't register, even though this had to be Tori's fifth time saying them. She glared at her fiancé, still desperately trying to come to terms with the information her mother had blasted to everyone at the packed Thanksgiving dinner table.

"Seriously? How is that even humanly possible when you didn't know the woman four hours ago?" Tori shouted.

"Tori, 1-let me explain," Dallas stammered.

Twelve pairs of eyes were now focused on the not-quite-blissful couple standing at the bottom of the stairs just off from the dining room.

"But not here. Let's go somewhere and talk. I'm telling you, it's not what you think."

"What did you do?" Tori snapped, glaring up at Dallas. "Trip over the sheets, and your penis somehow landed in a woman nearly twice my age?"

The drumstick in Uncle Bill's hand paused in midair on its journey to his wide mouth. Cousin Tiny's fleshy hand flew to her overexposed bosom and came to rest somewhere above her heart. Even Tori's father's frozen expression of alarm would have been Three Stooges comical if the situation weren't so tragic.

Aunt Yoli was the first to recover. "Did they just say what I think they said?"

In unison, everyone nodded.

"Girl, shut the front door and run out the back!"

A few bursts of nervous laughter sprang up around the table, but they were not nearly enough to chase away the unease that had flooded the room when Tori stepped into the house. She'd gone to drop off Aunt Rose's drunk self at home. Tori hadn't even been in the house good when her mother, Bernice, blurted out that she'd caught Alicia and Dallas together. Alone. In bed. In the nude. Tori had picked up from there and summed it up in one sweep. "You slept with my aunt ..."

"Nothing happened, Tori," Dallas said, his voice shaky. "I didn't sleep with her."

"So, my mama's lying?" Tori asked.

128

Dallas shifted uneasily.

"Hell no. I know what I saw," Bernice snapped. She had moved from the dining room table to the end of the staircase, right next to her daughter, poised as if she was ready to go to battle. "Both of you were in bed butt-ass naked." She jabbed angrily in her sister-in-law's direction.

Alicia hadn't moved from her spot at the top of the staircase. Probably because she knew what was best for her. "She was butt-naked. And he was nut-naked," Bernice yelled. "Wasn't an inch of space between them." She flickered a gaze at Dallas. "Look at him. You can tell he just got dressed."

Tori closed her eyes and took deep breaths to calm the emotions that warred within her.

"See, I told you Alicia wasn't worth a damn," Bernice crowed with savage satisfaction. "And looks like Mr. NBA ain't much better. You thought he was all that and a side order of fries."

Dallas Avery was the NBA's most valuable player, and a man most women would give their right and left ovary to call their own. But Most Eligible Bachelor or not, he had set Tori's bitch meter into overdrive. Even with his chiseled, handsome face, towering muscular frame and million-dollar bank accounts, he was now worth next to nothing in her eyes. Too bad her aching heart didn't get that memo.

Tori didn't know if she was more enraged or hurt that her mother had been all too willing to drive this stake through her own daughter's heart in order to publicly disgrace Alicia.

"Tori, we need to talk about this," Dallas repeated before adding, "in private."

Bernice wore a satisfied smirk as she glared openly up at Alicia, who just kept staring stoically at them from the second floor landing. "The angel of the family has fallen," Bernice said.

"Hey, Bernice," Bill taunted with a hearty chuckle. "Bet you won't say that when Alicia comes downstairs. You know she's gonna put a hurting on you."

"You mean put *another* hurting on her," Aunt Yoli added, doubling over with laughter.

Tori wanted to scream. Her life was unraveling in front of her and her family was cracking jokes.

Instinctively, Bernice inched away from the staircase and back toward the dining room table. Her hands went up to the small scar on her neck, probably remembering that a year ago on this very same holiday, Alicia had ended a vicious blow-for-blow fight with a knife at Bernice's throat. Almost gave the woman a "Sicilian Smile"—an ear-to-ear slice across the throat.

Dallas reached for Tori's hand. "It's not what it seems."

She snatched away, parted her lips to give him what was left of her mind, but Cousin Tiny chimed in first. "Alicia had every right to take Bernice to the floor last year for that foul mess she said. I would've pulled out my own can of whoop ass behind that one."

Tiny's husband, Thomas, nodded his watermelon-sized head.

The rest of the family finally sprang to life, also chiming in all at once to defend Alicia, the one woman everyone could count on in a time of need, to lend an ear when it was called for and to dry a tear when no one else bothered to care. That she would do something as low as sleep with her niece's soon-to-be husband was unthinkable. So the family sidestepped that issue for as long as they could, finding it more comfortable to speak on the reason no one had expected Alicia home for Thanksgiving— especially since none of them had heard from her for an entire year.

Dallas maneuvered so he was in front of Tori. "Nothing. Happened."

"If Bernice had said that bull to me," Bill responded, still trying to tackle the last of the drumstick, "an ass whipping would've been the least of her problems." He beckoned toward the last slice of sweet potato pie at the other end of the table. "That has my name written all over it."

"Bernice is lying," Martha said. "Alicia's still got looks and all, but that young stud wouldn't pick her over Tori." She shot an appreciative glance toward Dallas, then leaned to her right and whispered loudly in Yoli's direction, "But girl, he is finer than frog's hair."

Yoli gave him a lusty once-over. "I'd give him some my damn self.

He's the type of man who can make a woman put a for sale sign on one thigh and an open for business sign on the other. Yes, Lawd."

Tori tried her best to tune out her family. She didn't have the stamina to deal with them right now. "How could you do this? You're my fiancé."

"You're Tori's fiancé?" Alicia finally spoke out. She eased down the stairs, looking first to Tori then to Dallas. Her panic-stricken expression gave Tori pause. Could her aunt really have not known?

Alicia turned back to her niece. "Oh, my, God, Tori. I had no idea. I'm so, so sorry." She didn't give Tori time to reply as she brushed past Dallas, slipped into the nearest pair of shoes—her brother's—and ran out of the front door, oblivious to the fact that she barely had on enough clothing to protect her from the chill in the room, let alone the sub-zero temps of a Chicago winter.

The whole crowd gasped in disbelief as Dallas grabbed his leather coat from the foyer closet. "She can't go out there with nothing on," he said as he stepped into his Timberlands. "I'll be right back."

Tori was ready to spit fire. "Are you kidding me?" she screamed as he quickly laced up his shoes, then darted toward the door. "You're going after my aunt? My aunt," she yelled, following him. "My heart is bleeding all over the carpet and you're going after her!"

The front door slammed and Tori stood frozen, unable to believe what happened in the last ten minutes. Bernice's voice snapped Tori out of her trance. "Girl, I taught you better than that," Bernice yelled, gesturing to the door. "You'd better go get your man!"

About Open Door Marriage

USA TODAY Bestselling Author, Naleighna Kai, tells the dynamic love triangle of a chance encounter that lands wealthy NBA star, Dallas Avery, back in the arms of Alicia, the woman of his dreams. A woman he hasn't seen in years. A woman he soon discovers is his fiancée's long-lost aunt!

But Tori, isn't ready to give up all that she's worked for in their relationship, so she makes him a shocking offer—go through with the wedding and she'll still allow him to be with the one woman he now can't seem to do without. Dallas will get a family, something her aunt can't give him and Tori will have the lifestyle she clamors. And Alicia will embrace the love she's longed for all her life and that had already been in her reach before she disappeared. Everyone will get a little of what they want. . . and maybe a whole lot of what they don't.

The details of the trio's love life play out in the tabloids and on talk shows, making Dallas the center of an NBA scandal. Eventually, the doors slam shut on this open marriage in the making and Dallas is forced to make a choice to end the chaos. Unfortunately, moving on is easier than it looks and by the time all is said and done, secrets will be revealed, passions will be extinguished, and everyone's lives will be forever changed.

ABOUT YVONNE ELLIOTT

Yvonne Elliott, is the talented author hailing from the city of Chicago, Illinois. Her journey in the literary world has been nothing short of extraordinary.

In 2022, Yvonne's debut memoir *"Rebirth: Rising out of the Shadows and into the Light,"* took the world by storm. It soared to become Amazon #1 New Release and earned her the esteemed title of #1 Best-Selling Author in not just one, but two categories. A remarkable achievement, indeed.

Yvonne's life has been shaped by her rich experiences, as she served as an Air Force veteran for an impressive twenty-two years. It was during her teenage years that she discovered her passion for writing. Poetry and short stories became her outlet to process the complexities of the world around her.

Beyond her writing prowess, Yvonne is an integral part of the NK Tribe Called Success, where she serves as one of the group's in-house bookkeeper, contributing to the groups collective growth and empowerment.

When not immersed in her writing world, Yvonne finds joy in the company of her loving husband and two beautiful children. Her serene moments are spent in the embrace of her garden or embarking on exciting journeys with her closest friends.

Get ready for her upcoming creation, "A Night To Remember," set to captivate hearts as her first venture into romantic fiction. Teaming up with USA Today Bestselling Author, Naleighna Kai, this collaboration promises an unforgettable sensual experience for readers.

Stay in touch with Yvonne Elliott and be part of her literary adventures by joining her mailing list. Enjoy exclusive book updates, exciting giveaways, and insights into her creative process on her blog. Connect with Yvonne at www.authoryvonneelliott.com

Experience the magic of Yvonne Elliott's storytelling and be swept away on a journey of emotions and imagination. Don't miss out on this rising literary star!

ABOUT NALEIGHNA KAI

Naleighna Kai is the *USA TODAY, Essence®,* and national bestselling and award-winning author of several women's fiction, contemporary fiction, Christian fiction, romance, erotica, and science fiction novels that plumb the depth of unique relationships and women's issues. She is also a contributor to a *New York Times* bestseller, one of AALBC's 100 Top Authors, a member of the CVS Hall of Fame, a Mercedes Benz Mentor Award Nominee, and the recipient of the E. Lynn Harris Author of Distinction award.

She continues to "pay it forward" by organizing the annual Cavalcade of Authors which gives readers intimate access to the most accomplished writing talent today. She also established and heads up the NK Tribe Called Success, which offers aspiring and established authors assistance with ghostwriting, developmental editing, publishing, marketing, and other services to jump-start or enhance their writing careers. https://bit.ly/NaleighnaKai